I0600443

Oh, Promise Me!

A Farce in Three Acts

by Pete Williams

A SAMUEL FRENCH ACTING EDITION

SAMUEL FRENCH

FOUNDED 1830

New York Hollywood London Toronto

SAMUELFRENCH.COM

Copyright © 1939 by Samuel French
Copyright © 1967 by James Reach

ALL RIGHTS RESERVED

CAUTION: Professionals and amateurs are hereby warned that *OH, PROMISE ME!* is subject to a Licensing Fee. It is fully protected under the copyright laws of the United States of America, the British Commonwealth, including Canada, and all other countries of the Copyright Union. All rights, including professional, amateur, motion picture, recitation, lecturing, public reading, radio broadcasting, television and the rights of translation into foreign languages are strictly reserved. In its present form the play is dedicated to the reading public only.

The amateur live stage performance rights to *OH, PROMISE ME!* are controlled exclusively by Samuel French, Inc., and licensing arrangements and performance licenses must be secured well in advance of presentation. PLEASE NOTE that amateur Licensing Fees are set upon application in accordance with your producing circumstances. When applying for a licensing quotation and a performance license please give us the number of performances intended, dates of production, your seating capacity and admission fee. Licensing Fees are payable one week before the opening performance of the play to Samuel French, Inc., at 45 W. 25th Street, New York, NY 10010.

Licensing Fee of the required amount must be paid whether the play is presented for charity or gain and whether or not admission is charged.

Stock licensing fees quoted upon application to Samuel French, Inc.

For all other rights than those stipulated above, apply to: Samuel French, Inc.

Particular emphasis is laid on the question of amateur or professional readings, permission and terms for which must be secured in writing from Samuel French, Inc.

Copying from this book in whole or in part is strictly forbidden by law, and the right of performance is not transferable.

Whenever the play is produced the following notice must appear on all programs, printing and advertising for the play: "Produced by special arrangement with Samuel French, Inc."

Due authorship credit must be given on all programs, printing and advertising for the play.

No one shall commit or authorize any act or omission by which the copyright of, or the right to copyright, this play may be impaired.
No one shall make any changes in this play for the purpose of production.
Publication of this play does not imply availability for performance. Both amateurs and professionals considering a production are strongly advised in their own interests to apply to Samuel French, Inc., for written permission before starting rehearsals, advertising, or booking a theatre.
No part of this book may be reproduced, stored in a retrieval system, or transmitted in any form, by any means, now known or yet to be invented, including mechanical, electronic, photocopying, recording, videotaping, or otherwise, without the prior written permission of the publisher.

ISBN   978-0-573-60241-2   Printed   in   U.S.A.   #17901

OH, PROMISE ME!

STORY OF THE PLAY

As an inducement to laughter, we know of no finer play in recent seasons than this jolly, rollicking, swift-moving new farce by Mr. Williams. Besides a very full quota of hilarity, you will find also in this play apt characterizations, zestful dialogue, plausible situations, and a wealth of action, color and incident. Barry Hollis, at twenty-one, has just graduated from Princeton, thereby coming into the fortune left him in his late father's will. His youthful escapades have won him a reputation as a playboy, but he is resolved to settle down now and become a worthy member of the community. On the train back from Princeton he meets and falls immediately in love with Gladys Vance. He persuades his aunt, with whom he makes his home, to send Gladys a note inviting her for a visit. Another note goes to Patsie Linden, a hard-boiled little dancer and old flame of Barry's, asking her to send back his frat pin. Alas, the notes get mixed! Patsie arrives with her mother, an ex-burlesque queen, and threatens a breach of promise suit unless Barry marries her immediately. Then Barry has a bright idea: He couldn't possibly marry Patsie if he had a wife and family already. So he gets Ann Furber, the butler's daughter, to pretend to be his wife—and to make it more convincing, he "borrows" a strange baby. Into this situation marches Gladys, the light of his life, and Barry's in an awful pickle! He's got to convince Patsie he *is* married and Gladys he *isn't* married at

3

the same time. From this point, complication piles on complication with bewildering rapidity—with a surprise on every page, and a laugh in every line. The climax comes when Barry is arrested for kidnaping the baby. Then, to top this, he is informed that his estate has dwindled to almost nothing, and all his girl-friends desert him—that is, all except one. Who she is we won't divulge here, but she helps bring the play to a surprising finish amid a whirlwind of laughter. Here's a farce easy to stage and cast, and with never an offensive line. We recommend it strongly to high schools, churches, and all other amateur groups.

CHARACTERS
(In order of appearance)

SETH MILLER, *a lawyer*
FURBER, *a butler*
BARRY HOLLIS, *a young millionaire*
MRS. SUE HOLLIS, *his aunt*
JUNE HOLLIS, *his young sister*
KATHLEEN, *the cook*
ANN FURBER, *a young actress*
PATSIE LINDEN, *a dancer*
MRS. LINDEN, *her mother*
GLADYS VANCE, *a dream-girl*
RALPH SAUNDERS, *a man with a purpose*
MRS. JONES, *a young mother*

SYNOPSIS OF ACTS

*The action of the entire play takes place in the living
room of the Hollis home, in a small mid-Western
city.*

ACT I:
   SCENE I: *The present. Late afternoon on a
                June day.*
   SCENE II: *Several days later. Early evening.*

ACT II: *The same night. About half an hour later.*

ACT III: *The same night. About two hours later.*

5

DESCRIPTION OF CHARACTERS

MILLER *is a man of forty. Prosperous looking, and he has a commanding appearance. Is inclined to be pompous and to carry his courtroom manner into his private life.*

FURBER *is a man of forty-five. Has a certain distinction and perfect manners. Never raises his voice above an ordinary conversational tone. In the first scene, he wears a white coat and dark trousers, in other scenes, a tail coat and black tie.*

BARRY *is a young man of twenty-one. He is very good-looking, well-groomed and shows good breeding. Has a certain cockiness of manner and shows that he has been accustomed to getting what he wants, but his personality is ingratiating. He is quick and nervous in his actions and a rapid talker.*

MRS. HOLLIS *is a woman of thirty-five. She makes a very handsome appearance and dresses exceedingly well. She has intelligence, poise and a nice personality.*

JUNE *is a girl of seventeen. She is charming in a rather immature way, has intelligence and a good sense of humor. Dresses informally but well.*

KATHLEEN *is a young woman of twenty-five. Unmistakably Irish in appearance and talks with quite a thick brogue. Wears a white dress and apron.*

7

ANN *is a girl of nineteen. She is slight of stature and has a great deal of whispy charm; intelligent and well-poised. Wears a plain but becoming dress.*

PATSIE *is a girl of twenty-one. Very attractive in a flamboyant way. Wears loud, flashy clothes. A "show-girl" type.*

MRS. LINDEN *is a woman of fifty. Tries to make herself look younger; her clothes and manner are both rather vulgar. Has the mark of "show business" upon her.*

GLADYS *is a girl of nineteen. Very attractive appearance; well-dressed and has poise, but there is a certain haughtiness about her manner.*

> NOTE: ANN, PATSIE *and* GLADYS *should be played by three girls of distinctly different types.*

RALPH *is a young man of twenty-five. The athletic type; burly and formidable in appearance.*

MRS. JONES *is a young woman of twenty-five. Very excitable and with a shrill voice.*

OH, PROMISE ME!

ACT ONE

Scene I

THE TIME: *The present; late afternoon on a June day.*

THE PLACE: *The living room of the Hollis home in a small mid-Western city. The room is furnished richly and in the modern manner. The furniture is new, modernistic in design, and the room should convey the impression of wealthy owners. The main entrance is a large archway midway of the back wall. This leads on the Left to the front door, and on the Right to the stairway, neither of which needs to be visible to the audience. Two doors in the Right wall: Right 1 leads to kitchen and dining room; Right 2 leads to the den. Two windows in the Left wall. Against the Left wall, between the windows, a desk and desk chair; on the desk a telephone. Center a divan; in front of it a coffee table. Two armchairs, each with end-table and table lamp, down Right and Left respectively. Another armchair in the corner up Left. A library table against Right wall between the two doors. On the library table a large pottery vase. Two torchieres against back wall, Right and Left of*

*arch. Outside the arch, against the hall back-
ing, a console table with mirror hanging above
it. Pictures, books, ashtrays, etc.*

AT RISE: FURBER *and* MILLER *are discovered.* FUR-
BER *is arranging some fresh flowers in the vase
on the library table.* MILLER *is pacing up and
down impatiently.*

MILLER. *(After a moment, stops upstage, takes
out a watch and looks at it)* Wish he'd hurry.

FURBER. *(Arranging the flowers)* They can't be
much longer, sir.

MILLER. Yes, I know, I know. But I've got an
office—and a client waiting for me. It's after four
now.

FURBER. The train wasn't due until five minutes
of, sir—and it takes fifteen minutes to drive from
the station.

MILLER. Uh! *(Resumes pacing; after another moment)* You're sure he *is* coming straight here, Furber?

FURBER. Why, that was my understanding, Mr.
Miller. Mrs. Hollis said they'd come directly home
from the station.

MILLER. Well— *(Looks at watch again)* I'll give
them five minutes more. I can't let my whole prac-
tise go to boot waiting for them.

FURBER. Yes, sir. *(Finishing with the flowers,
crosses up to arch)* Can I get you anything while
you're waiting, Mr. Miller?

MILLER. No, thanks.

FURBER. *(Crosses to desk and gets a newspaper)*
Perhaps you'd like to see this afternoon's paper—it
just came, sir.

MILLER. Oh, much obliged, Furber. *(Takes it
from him; looks at it)* Well! Got the story in here
already, eh?

FURBER. Have they, sir? I haven't looked at it.

MILLER. Yes. *(Reads)* "Young Socialite Comes Into Large Inheritance Today. Barry Hollis, twenty-one, whose father, the late Edgar G. Hollis, was founder of the local Hollis Mills, will arrive here this afternoon after his recent graduation from Princeton University. According to the terms of his father's will, young Hollis, whose irrepressible pranks have won him the reputation of being one of the country's leading playboys, will today become the legal custodian of the sizable Hollis fortune—"

(DOORBELL rings.)

FURBER. *(Looking out window, somewhat excited)* It's Mr. Barry now! Excuse me, sir— *(Exits c. to L. His voice is heard from offstage)* Welcome home, sir!

BARRY. *(Offstage)* Thanks, you old-stick-in-the-mud! *(Enters c. from L., followed by MRS. HOLLIS and FURBER. The latter is carrying several pieces of luggage.)*

MILLER. Hello, young man!

BARRY. Oh, how are you, Mr. Miller? *(Looks around)* Well, well—old place hasn't changed much, has it?

MRS. HOLLIS. You're as unobservant as ever. The furniture is almost completely new.

BARRY. Is it? Oh, well—furniture always looks alike to me.

MILLER. How've you been, Barry? How's the East?

BARRY. Fine, fine! *(Crosses to FURBER; digs him playfully in the ribs)* You haven't changed, have you? Furber, you never seem to get a day older.

FURBER. Thank you, Mr. Barry. Shall I take these bags up to your room?

BARRY. Yeah. And lay out some towels and stuff—

I want to take a shower after that dusty train trip.

FURBER. Very good, sir. *(Exits* C. *to* R. *with the bags.)*

BARRY. How about a bite to eat, Aunt Sue?

MRS. HOLLIS. Dinner will be at seven—

BARRY. Sure, I know—but I'm starved. Be a good girl and see what you can rustle up—sandwich, or something.

MRS. HOLLIS. *(Sighs)* Same old Barry! I'll speak to Kathleen. *(Crosses, opens door* R.1 *and calls)* Kathleen!

BARRY. Who's she?

MRS. HOLLIS. Kathleen? The new cook. Don't you remember I wrote you about Eliza leaving to get married?

BARRY. Oh, yeah! How's this one—know how to cook corned beef and cabbage? *(To* MILLER*)* My favorite fruit.

KATHLEEN. *(Enters* R.1*)* Did you want me, Mrs. Hollis?

MRS. HOLLIS. Yes. Kathleen, this is my nephew, Barry.

BARRY. *(Waves a hand at her)* How are you, Kathleen?

KATHLEEN. Sure, I'm glad to make your acquaintance, sir.

MRS. HOLLIS. Mr. Barry will be living with us, and it's only fair to warn you he's a tremendous eater, Kathleen.

KATHLEEN. Is he now, ma'am—?

BARRY. Especially corned beef and cabbage—and I hope you're good at it, Kathleen.

KATHLEEN. Corned beef and cabbage, is it? *(Smiles and nods)* Now did you ever know a Mick that wasn't, sir?

MRS. HOLLIS. See if you can find anything in the refrigerator for a sandwich. I believe there's some of that cold chicken left, isn't there?

(KATHLEEN nods "yes"; turns to exit.)

BARRY. And coffee, Kathleen—oodles of coffee.

KATHLEEN. Yes, sir. Oodles of coffee it is, sir. *(Exits R.I.)*

MRS. HOLLIS. Well, why are we all standing? *(Crosses to chair R.)* Have a seat, Seth. *(Motions him to divan and sits.)*

MILLER. *(Who has been perusing paper, now folds it and places it back on desk)* No, thanks, Sue. I've a client waiting in my office. I wanted to have a word with Barry.

BARRY. Me, Mr. Miller?

MILLER. Yes. Young man, your graduation from Princeton means that you've completed your part of the bargain according to the terms of your father's will. And now—

BARRY. And now—I become— *(Grimaces in distaste)* "A malefactor of great wealth."

MILLER. Not necessarily. There are great opportunities today to make your money count for something—something really worthwhile.

MRS. HOLLIS. *(Nods)* Exactly what I've been telling him.

MILLER. I trust, now that you have—ah—reached your maturity, you are ready to settle down and become a useful citizen—

BARRY. Oh, sure. Solid as can be. Wife, family—and all that sort of thing.

MILLER. Exactly! This has been a great responsibility to me. And now that it's over—

MRS. HOLLIS. *(Frowning)* What did you say, Barry—a *wife?*

BARRY. *(Carelessly)* Oh, just a figure of speech, Aunt Sue. Go on, Mr. Miller.

MILLER. Yes. As I was saying, now that my trusteeship has been completed, I should like to give you an accounting as soon as convenient—

BARRY. Why bother about it? Can't we just go on as we have been doing—?

MILLER. No. The will distinctly specifies that you shall take over the active management of the estate.

BARRY. *(Sighs)* I'm so bad at figures.

MILLER. You'll learn, no doubt. *(Crosses to arch)* I'll expect you at my office tomorrow—

BARRY. *(Crossing up to arch with him)* Not tomorrow! Have a heart, Mr. Miller—my first day in town? Make it next week.

MILLER. Next week? H'mmm! *(Frowns)* Very well, the first part of the week. I believe I have Tuesday morning available.

BARRY. Oke! See you then.

MILLER. Yes. Of course, if there is any way in which I can help—

BARRY. *(Ushering him into arch)* Thanks—thanks —I'll remember that.

MILLER. *(Gets his hat from console table)* And if you'll permit me to say so, I trust for your aunt's sake and your own, young man, that you have outgrown your—ah—"playboy" habits—

BARRY. *(Anxious to be rid of him)* Sure! I'm a new man—you'll see—industrious as a beaver! Goodbye, Mr. Miller—see you Tuesday.

MILLER. Yes. Goodbye! Goodbye, Sue! *(Exits c. to L.)*

BARRY. Whoo! Stuffy old coot, isn't he? *(Comes down to her.)*

MRS. HOLLIS. Seth is a very able lawyer—very able indeed. Your father had implicit confidence in his judgment—

BARRY. Sure, sure, I know. But he's still dry as dust. *(Sits on arm of her chair and playfully ruffles her hair)* Good old Aunt Sue!

MRS. HOLLIS. Barry! *(Slaps at him)* I spent hours on my hair this morning, and now you've made a wreck of it—

BARRY. Don't worry. Now that I'm an "Economic Royalist," I can buy you a couple of beauty parlors.

MRS. HOLLIS. Seth Miller was right, Barry. I do hope you've put your—your boyhood days behind you—

BARRY. Don't you worry your pretty head about it. I'm the man of the family now. See?

MRS. HOLLIS. I hope so.

BARRY. Sure. And to prove it to you, I'm— *(Rises from chair. Casually)* going to get married.

MRS. HOLLIS. *(Astounded) What!*

BARRY. Why not? A wife's the best cure for "play-boy-itis," don't you think?

MRS. HOLLIS. Barry—you're not *serious?*

BARRY. You bet! Just wait'll you see her, Aunt Sue. She's glorious! She's gorgeous! She's glamorous! She's—

MRS. HOLLIS. *(Sighs helplessly)* What's her name?

BARRY. Perfect! Absolutely— What did you say?

MRS. HOLLIS. I said, what's her name?

BARRY. Her name? Oh—er— *(Frowns)* Let me see—

MRS. HOLLIS. *(Laughs ironically)* This absolutely perfect creature—you're going to marry her, and yet you don't know her name.

BARRY. *(Indignant)* Who doesn't? It's—er— *(Grins triumphantly)* Gladys! Gladys Vance! And no kidding, Aunt Sue, she's the loveliest thing this side of Paradise—

MRS. HOLLIS. How long have you known her?

BARRY. She's— How long have I known her? Oh, just a few hours. But she's one in a million. She's—

MRS. HOLLIS. *A few hours?*

BARRY. *(Smiles brightly)* Uh-huh! I met her on the train. Her window was stuck and I opened it for her—

MRS. HOLLIS. *(Sarcastically)* Well, of course, that explains everything, doesn't it?

BARRY. Now, don't be a killjoy, Aunt Sue. You'll love her—she's got everything—everything!

MRS. HOLLIS. Including you, apparently.

BARRY. You bet! I'm hers, to have and to hold, till death do us— *(Suddenly)* Oh! Before I forget— *(Crosses to telephone; starts to dial a number.)*

MRS. HOLLIS. What are you doing?

BARRY. Calling the tailor to order a morning coat —for the wedding, you know.

MRS. HOLLIS. Just a minute! That can wait.

BARRY. Oh, well— *(Shrugs)* I suppose it can. *(Hangs up and comes back across to her.)*

MRS. HOLLIS. Does this—this *dream-girl* of yours live here in town?

BARRY. Oh, no. She's from the East—er—Boston, I think. She's on her way to visit a friend in Park-town.

MRS. HOLLIS. And does she *know* she's to have the dubious honor of being your wife?

BARRY. No-o, not yet. But she expects to be free next week, and she promised me she'd come here for a visit if you invited her.

MRS. HOLLIS. *(Snorts)* Huh! Very kind of her, I'm sure—but of course I'll do nothing of the kind.

BARRY. *(Smiles knowingly)* Oh, yes, you will, my dear Aunt Sue—oh, yes, you will!

MRS. HOLLIS. Why should I invite some strange girl about whom you apparently know nothing except that she can't open train windows?

BARRY. Because you've got a weak heart, and I don't think you could stand the shock of a sudden elopement.

MRS. HOLLIS. *(Aghast)* Elopement? Barry, you wouldn't!

BARRY. Of course not. It's the last thing I want to do—unless I *have* to.

MRS. HOLLIS. *(Sighs in acceptance of the inevitable)* What's her address?

BARRY. I've got it somewhere. You just write the note, and I'll take care of mailing it. *(Pats her head)* Good old Aunt Sue! I knew I could count on you. And you won't regret it. Wait till you see her—just wait—

MRS. HOLLIS. I will.

BARRY. Her personality—so fresh, so charming, so—so agreeable!

MRS. HOLLIS. And I suppose that agreeability had nothing whatever to do with the fact that you're about to inherit several million dollars?

BARRY. *(Indignant)* How can you even *suggest* such a thing? It's sacrilegious! She's not that type at all—not—er—not Gladys!

MRS. HOLLIS. *(Dryly)* I seem to have been here before. This time it's Gladys. Before that it was—what was her name?—Patsie, wasn't it?

BARRY. *(Suddenly)* Omigosh!

MRS. HOLLIS. What's the matter?

BARRY. Patsie Linden! I've got to call it off—

MRS. HOLLIS. Call what off? What are you talking about?

BARRY. Well, you see, I—er—I sort of invited her and Mrs. Linden for a visit—

MRS. HOLLIS. It seems to me we could have a very profitable business here, by turning this house into a hotel for your "dream girls."

BARRY. "Ex-dream girls," if you're referring to Patsie. She can't hold a candle to Gladys.

MRS. HOLLIS. Well, you'd better do something about that invitation.

BARRY. Yeah, I'll drop her a line calling it off. That reminds me— She's got my frat pin. I'll have to ask her to send it back.

MRS. HOLLIS. Your frat pin? I thought you ordered half a dozen of them from the jewelers?

BARRY. Sure I did—but they're all gone. This is the last one, and I want Gladys to have it.

MRS. HOLLIS. But where did the others all go to?

BARRY. Oh, well— *(Shrugs vaguely)* You know how it is, Aunt Sue.

MRS. HOLLIS. *(Looks at him; shakes her head helplessly)* Yes, I believe I do. So you're going to be as industrious as a beaver? At what—opening train windows for pretty girls?

JUNE. *(Rushing in C. from L.)* Did he get here, Aunt Sue?

BARRY. Hello, Sis!

JUNE. Barry! Gosh, you're really back!

BARRY. In the flesh. *(Looking her over)* Say, what've you done to yourself?

JUNE. Done to myself? What do you mean?

BARRY. A kid your age—dressed up like that—

JUNE. *(Indignant)* Well, I like that!

MRS. HOLLIS. June is seventeen, Barry.

BARRY. No! *(Whistles wonderingly)* What do you know! Time certainly does fly, doesn't it? I thought you were about twelve, or something like that.

JUNE. You'd better wake up to the facts of life, big brother.

BARRY. Yeah, I guess I better had. *(Still looks at her almost unbelievingly.)*

FURBER. *(Enters C. from R.)* Beg pardon. Everything's ready for your shower now, Mr. Barry.

BARRY. Oke! It won't take me long— *(Crosses to arch)* Oh, Furber, the cook's making some coffee for me. Tell her to keep it hot till I finish upstairs.

FURBER. I will, Mr. Barry. *(Exits R.1.)*

BARRY. Better get busy on that note to Gladys, Aunt Sue. I want to mail it right away. *(Exits C. to R.)*

JUNE. *(As MRS. HOLLIS rises and crosses to R.2)* Who's Gladys, Aunt Sue?

MRS. HOLLIS. *(Sighs)* The latest in a long line of dream girls.

JUNE. *(Blinks uncomprehendingly)* Huh?

MRS. HOLLIS. She's a girl your brother met on a railroad train and wants to marry.

JUNE. *Marry?* Honestly, Aunt Sue?

MRS. HOLLIS. So he believes at the moment. But perhaps he'll change his mind. It's been known to happen before.

JUNE. He's awfully fickle, isn't he? He's had at least three girls that I know of.

MRS. HOLLIS. Three? You flatter him, June. *(As FURBER enters R.1)* Will you get several sheets of my notepaper and bring them to the den, Furber?

FURBER. There's some in there, Mrs. Hollis—in the drawer of your desk.

MRS. HOLLIS. Are you sure?

FURBER. Yes, ma'am. I placed it there the other day.

MRS. HOLLIS. Very well. *(Exits R.2.)*

FURBER. *(Crossing up to arch)* The paper has come, Miss June, if you care to look at it. *(Points to desk.)*

JUNE. Thanks, Furber. *(Crosses and gets it.)*

FURBER. You're welcome, Miss. *(Exits C. to R.)*

(JUNE crosses and sits in divan, opens newspaper and begins to read it.)

KATHLEEN. *(After a moment enters R.1, wheeling in a teatable on which are some sandwiches, cup and saucer, cream and sugar)* I'm keeping the coffee on the stove for your brother.

JUNE. All right.

KATHLEEN. He's the handsome one, ain't he, Miss June?

JUNE. Barry? Do you think he is?

KATHLEEN. Oh, that I do for fair, Miss.

JUNE. I've never really noticed.

KATHLEEN. *(Sighs)* He reminds me somewhat of my Percival.

JUNE. Percival? He's the one who left you waiting at the altar?

KATHLEEN. No, Miss—not at the altar,. 'Twas on our honeymoon he vanished. We was at Niagara Falls, and I went out to get some postcards to send to my family. When I got back to the hotel, my Percival had vanished—into thin air, you might say, Miss. I've never set eyes on him since.

JUNE. *(She's heard this story before. Murmurs)* Interesting.

KATHLEEN. I'm thinking we'll meet up again one of these days—and a sorry day that'll be for his black soul, bad cess to it.

JUNE. I shouldn't wonder.

KATHLEEN. But he was the pretty one, was Percival, Miss—as smooth as satin, and butter wouldn't melt in his mouth, you'd 've thought. *(Sighs)* Ah—he had a way with him, that he did.

JUNE. *(Gives up trying to read; smiles)* What'll you do if you *do* find him, Kathleen?

KATHLEEN. What'll I do, Miss? *(Fiercely)* I'll kill him, that I will—I'll kill him dead. *(Sighs soulfully)* Or kiss him. That's the trouble, I ain't sure which—he's that pretty, is my Percival.

(JUNE *laughs.*)

MRS. HOLLIS. *(Enters* R.2 *with sheet of notepaper)* That's done.

KATHLEEN. Oh, I got the sandwiches ready for Mr. Barry, ma'am. And the coffee's keeping hot. You let me know when he's ready for it.

MRS. HOLLIS. Very well, Kathleen.

KATHLEEN. I suppose, with this snack now, he won't be after wanting dinner till late tonight?

MRS. HOLLIS. Oh, yes, he will—you don't know his appetite. Dinner at the usual hour—seven.

KATHLEEN. Yes, ma'am. *(Exits R.1.)*

MRS. HOLLIS. *(Places note on the desk)* There! She's been invited. Now we shall see what a dream girl looks like in the flesh.

JUNE. Did he really meet her on the train, Aunt Sue?

MRS. HOLLIS. Yes. The technique of the stuck window seems to be quite a successful one.

JUNE. And so romantic. Won't it be priceless if he *does* marry her?

MRS. HOLLIS. I shouldn't place any bets on that, if I were you, June. *(Comes down and sits in chair L.)*

JUNE. Are you going to *do* something about it, Aunt Sue?

MRS. HOLLIS. *(Innocently)* Me? Why, what could I do about it? *(Smiles)* You ask too many questions, young lady.

JUNE. I get it. That's why you were so willing to invite her—so you can go to work on her when she gets here.

MRS. HOLLIS. I haven't said so. For all I know, she *may* be the gorgeous, wonderful, perfect person Barry describes her as being—

JUNE. Sure!

MRS. HOLLIS. But I doubt it.

JUNE. Oh, Aunt Sue—nearly forgot. I saw Ann Furber downtown.

MRS. HOLLIS. Really? When?

JUNE. Just a little while ago. Said she just got back from New York—probably on the same train Barry came on.

MRS. HOLLIS. How does she look?

JUNE. Gorgeous! You'd hardly know it was the same person.

MRS. HOLLIS. I understand she's quite a success on Broadway.

JUNE. That's what they say.

MRS. HOLLIS. I wonder if Furber knows she's here. He'll probably want the evening off—

BARRY. *(Enters c. from R. He is wearing a bathrobe, slippers and a towel around his neck)* Didn't take me long, did it?

JUNE. I should say not.

BARRY. Sandwiches! *(Crosses to tea wagon, picks one up and stuffs it into his mouth)* Good!

MRS. HOLLIS. Kathleen's keeping some coffee warm for you—

BARRY. *(Opens door R.1 and yells)* Kathleen! Coffee!

KATHLEEN. *(Off R.1)* Yes, sir!

BARRY. How about that note to Gladys, Aunt Sue?

MRS. HOLLIS. There it is. *(Points to desk.)*

BARRY. *(Crosses, picks it up and reads it)* Fine, Aunt Sue! This'll do the trick. Thanks a lot. *(Replaces it on desk, crosses and gets another sandwich.)*

MRS. HOLLIS. *(Rises)* I believe I'll lie down until dinner time— *(Crosses to arch)* I've a frightful headache. The excitement of getting ready for your return, Barry.

BARRY. Sure, take it easy, old girl.

MRS. HOLLIS. I'll see you at dinner. *(Exits c. to R.)*

KATHLEEN. *(Enters R.1 with percolator)* Here you are, Mr. Barry.

BARRY. Thanks, Kathleen.

KATHLEEN. You're welcome. *(Pours it into cup)* If you want some more, sir, just call me.

BARRY. Right.

(KATHLEEN *exits R.1 with percolator.)*

JUNE. Is she pretty, Barry?

BARRY. Gladys—pretty? No kidding, Sis, there just aren't words to describe her. But then, you wouldn't understand about those things.

JUNE. Oh, no?

BARRY. That reminds me—I'd better get that note off to Patsie—

JUNE. Patsie? Who's she?

BARRY. *(Takes his cup of coffee across to desk and sits down)* Oh, no one you know. *(Gets pen and paper; starts to write; frowns)* How would you go about telling a girl-friend it's all off?

JUNE. *(Shrugs)* Don't ask me! That's one thing I've never had to worry about.

BARRY. H'mm! *(Starts to write.)*

JUNE. Is that what you're doing?

BARRY. *(Writing)* Yeah—sort of.

JUNE. You ought to be pretty good at it by this time—you've had plenty of experience.

BARRY. *(After a moment)* How do you think this sounds? *(Reads)* "My dear Patsie, I find we're going to be very busy this summer, so won't have a chance to invite you, after all. If you get a chance to send my frat pin back, I'd like to have the jewelers replate it. Yours, Barry." How's it sound, Sis?

JUNE. It's certainly impersonal enough, if that's what you wanted.

BARRY. It is.

JUNE. If she ever had any hopes, that'll be the finish of them.

BARRY. I wonder. Patsie's a very strong-minded girl. And her mother—! Oh, well! I'd better get these off right away. *(Takes small address book from pocket of his robe; turns pages until he finds what he's looking for)* "Miss Gladys Vance, care of Henley, three-eleven Main Street, Parktown, Ohio." *(Takes envelope and addresses it.)*

JUNE. *(Rises)* I've got a date to watch a tennis match. *(Crosses to arch)* See you for dinner.

BARRY. All right, Sis.

JUNE. So long! *(Exits c. to L.)*

BARRY. *(Turns pages of address book again. Mur-*

murs as he writes another envelope) "Miss Patsie
Linden, six hundred Oakhurst Drive, Princeton, New
Jersey." *(Finishing the writing, he rises, picks up
the two notes and glances through them, folds them,
starts to place one in the envelope, carefully making
sure it is the correct one.)*

ANN. *(Enters R.I. She is dressed in street clothes.
As she sees him)* Oh, I *beg* your pardon! I didn't
think there was anyone in here— *(Turns to go.)*

BARRY. Just a minute! *(Looks at her interestedly;
puts letter down on desk)* I know you, don't I?

ANN. You're Barry Hollis, aren't you?

BARRY. I am.

ANN. I'm Ann Furber. Remember?

BARRY. *(Warmly)* Of course! *(Crosses to her)*
Little Ann Furber! Well, well! Long time no see,
eh?

ANN. Yes, it's been years, hasn't it?

BARRY. *(Looks her over admiringly)* No wonder
I didn't recognize you. You've certainly changed.

ANN. Not for the worse, I hope.

BARRY. Far from it! What have you been doing
and where have you keen keeping yourself?

ANN. Haven't you heard? I'm on the stage now—

BARRY. An actress? *(She nods)* What do you
know about that! *(WARN Curtain)*

ANN. I got in from New York this afternoon, to
spend the summer with my father.

BARRY. Does he know you're here?

ANN. Not yet, no. I was just looking for him.

BARRY. He's upstairs. I'll tell him.

ANN. Would you please, Mr. Hollis? I'll wait for
him out here.

BARRY. Oke! And don't keep yourself so strange
while you're around town.

ANN. I won't, thanks. *(Smiles and exits R.I.)*

BARRY. *(Looks after her for a moment, grinning,*

then crosses to arch and calls) Furber! *(Comes back to desk and, preoccupied with his thoughts about* ANN, *puts the notes into the wrong envelopes and seals them.)*

FURBER. *(Enters* c. *from* R.) Did you call me, Mr. Barry?

BARRY. I did. There's somebody waiting for you out there.

FURBER. *(His face lights up)* Ann, sir?

BARRY. Right! You old fraud—why didn't you tell me you had a beautiful daughter?

FURBER. She is nice, isn't she, sir?

BARRY. You bet! Well, look, I've got to get dressed— *(Crosses to arch)* Those letters—will you see that they get mailed as soon as possible?

FURBER. *(Crossing to desk)* Yes, sir. I'll take care of them right away, Mr. Barry—

BARRY. *(Exiting* c. *to* R.) Thanks!

FURBER. *(Picks up the letters)* I'll take care of them!

QUICK CURTAIN

ACT ONE

SCENE II

THE TIME: *Several days later. Early evening.*

THE PLACE: *The same.*

AT RISE: ANN *is discovered alone on stage. She is on divan, thoroughly relaxed, her head against the back of it.*

FURBER. *(After a moment, enters* R.I, *wheeling in the tea wagon, on which are two cups of coffee)*

Here we are! *(Places the cups on coffee table and sits in divan with her)*

ANN. Are you sure it's all right to have our coffee in here, Father?

FURBER. Certainly, my dear! The family won't be back until later. Mrs. Hollis and Mr. Barry were invited out to dinner, and Miss June has an engagement, I believe.

ANN. Kathleen certainly knows how to cook. Whoo! *(Sighs contentedly)* I haven't been so full in ages.

FURBER. I'm glad you enjoyed it, Ann.

ANN. I certainly did.

(They sip their coffee silently for a few moments.)

FURBER. It's nice having you back, my dear. We've had fun the last few days, haven't we?

ANN. Uh-huh! And we could go on having it always, Father, if you'd only—

FURBER. *(Cutting her short)* Now, Ann!

ANN. Well, why *won't* you, Father? You know it's silly for you to go on working as a butler when I'm earning enough to take care of both of us.

FURBER. You know how I feel about that, my dear. It's what I've been accustomed to, all my life, practically, and I shouldn't know what to do if I stopped—

ANN. There'd be plenty to do—

FURBER. Besides, the Hollises need me. They've been very good to me, and I shouldn't like to let them down.

ANN. *(Nods)* They *are* nice, aren't they?

FURBER. *(Leans over to put his cup on table)* Especially Mr. Barry, eh, my dear?

ANN. *(A little confused)* Why—what do you mean, Father?

FURBER. *(With a kindly smile)* Butlers are trained

to notice little things, Ann. You like him, don't you?

ANN. *(Rises)* Of course not! That is—well, I *like* him, but that's all.

FURBER. Sure?

ANN. *(With a little too much emphasis)* Certainly I'm sure! I've got my career to think of— *(An afterthought)* And besides, there's Ralph Sanders, isn't there?

FURBER. Ralph Sanders, your young man in New York—yes.

ANN. I'd be a fool to kid myself into thinking I could ever mean anything to Barry Hollis.

FURBER. That's right, my dear. Not that you're not good enough for him—you are. But Mr. Barry is—well, not too dependable.

ANN. I know that.

FURBER. A pity, too. He's such a fine young man in many ways. I'm afraid he's had too much money for his own good. *(Sighs)* So, my dear, the best thing you can do is forget him.

ANN. Don't be silly, Father. I've told you—there's nothing to forget.

FURBER. Well, that's all right, then— *(DOOR-BELL rings)* The bell— *(Rises)* These things—

ANN. I'll take care of them— *(They hurriedly put the cups back on tea wagon as the DOORBELL rings again)* You'd better answer it, Father.

FURBER. Have we got everything? *(Looks around to make sure, then crosses and exits C. to L., as ANN wheels the tea-wagon out R.I.)*

MRS. HOLLIS. *(Enters C. from L., followed by FURBER)* What kept you, Furber?

FURBER. I—er—I was just finishing my dinner, Mrs. Hollis.

MRS. HOLLIS. Oh! *(Crosses, sits in divan, rips her hat off and holds a hand to her head.)*

FURBER. Beg pardon, ma'am—are you feeling ill?

MRS. HOLLIS. One of my sick headaches. I had to excuse myself right after dinner.

FURBER. Shall I get you some aspirins, ma'am?

MRS. HOLLIS. Yes, I suppose I'd better have some, and lie down afterwards.

FURBER. Yes, ma'am. *(Starts to cross R. as DOORBELL rings.)*

MRS. HOLLIS. You'd better see who that is first.

FURBER. Very good, ma'am. *(Turns and exits C. to L.)*

PATSIE. *(Offstage)* Where's Barry?

FURBER. *(Offstage)* Mr. Hollis is not at home, Miss.

PATSIE. *(Offstage)* He ain't? Well, come on in, Mom—let's look the joint over. *(Enters C. from L., followed by* MRS. LINDEN *and* FURBER.*)*

MRS. HOLLIS. *(Startled, rises)* I beg your pardon—?

PATSIE. Hello! Who're you—Barry's old lady?

MRS. HOLLIS. Why—! I—er—I'm Sue Hollis. Isn't there—some mistake?

PATSIE. Oh, yeah—Aunt Sue! You're the one who sent us the invite.

MRS. HOLLIS. *(Looking from one to the other incredulously)* Are you—Gladys?

PATSIE. Gladys? Nope, the name is Patsie—Patsie Linden.

MRS. HOLLIS. Oh, Patsie! But—I don't understand—Barry wrote to you, didn't he—?

PATSIE. *(Annoyed)* Say, what is this? Barry didn't write to me. *You* did—

MRS. HOLLIS. *I?*

PATSIE. Yeah, you! I got the letter right here to prove it. *(Pats her purse)* And if you're trying to back out now, it's no soap. *(Indignant)* Why, you shouldn't do that, Aunt Sue. What would Barry think—?

MRS. HOLLIS. *(Beginning to see the light)* Yes—

that's right. What *would* he think? *(Half smiles to herself.)*

PATSIE. I'm his fiance-see, and you just better make up your mind to like it.

MRS. HOLLIS. Er—yes. Yes, of course— *(Bites her lip to keep back a smile)* I understand perfectly.

PATSIE. *(Appeased)* That's more like it. And this is my Mom—

MRS. HOLLIS. How do you do?

MRS. LINDEN. *(Waves a greeting)* How are you, dearie? Whoo! I'm all choked up and full of cinders. *(Looks about)* Say, you wouldn't have a shot of something around— (PATSIE *pokes her in the ribs)* Ouch! What'sa matter?

PATSIE. Act refined, Mom, act refined! You ain't in any dump now.

MRS. LINDEN. Well, what did I do—?

PATSIE. You got a buck and a half on you, Aunt Sue?

MRS. HOLLIS. A—buck and a half?

PATSIE. Uh-huh! For the cab—it's waiting outside.

MRS. HOLLIS. Oh! Of course. *(Opens purse, takes out bill and hands it to* FURBER) Pay the man off, Furber.

FURBER. Yes, Mrs. Hollis. *(Turns to exit.)*

MRS. LINDEN. Hey, Sonnie! Bring the bags in—

FURBER. Very good, madame.

MRS. LINDEN. And be careful of that little brown one. It's—it's got something in it.

(FURBER bows and exits C. to L.)

PATSIE. Where's Barry at?

MRS. HOLLIS. He's dining out, but he should be home very shortly.

PATSIE. Uh-huh! I was gonna let him know what

train we was making, but then I thought it'd be kinda nice to surprise him.

MRS. HOLLIS. Well, he'll certainly be surprised.

PATSIE. Yeah, that's what I figured.

MRS. HOLLIS. Shall we sit down?

PATSIE. Sure! *(She and* MRS. LINDEN *sit in divan.* MRS. HOLLIS *sits in chair* R.)

MRS. LINDEN. Golly! *(Winces)* Lemme get outa my shoe— *(Kicks one of her shoes off)* My corns is been givin' me Hail Columbia!

PATSIE. How many times I gotta tell you, Mom? Act refined, act refined!

MRS. LINDEN. Well, what's 'a matter with corns? We all got 'em—all us *old* dames—ain't that right, dearie?

MRS. HOLLIS. *(Smiles)* I know just what you mean.

MRS. LINDEN. *(Triumphantly to* PATSIE) See! When it comes to corns, we're all sisters under the skin.

MRS. HOLLIS. That's quite true.

MRS. LINDEN. Do you skin yours, dearie, or just coddle 'em along?

MRS. HOLLIS. *(Startled)* Well, really—I—

MRS. LINDEN. I always thought trimmin' 'em was best.

MRS. HOLLIS. I see.

MRS. LINDEN. *(Sighs)* Mine come from so much dancing—

MRS. HOLLIS. Er—dancing?

PATSIE. Now I suppose you're gonna tell her all about your past.

MRS. LINDEN. She means my burlesque days— twenty years as a featured dancer.

MRS. HOLLIS. Oh, really?

MRS. LINDEN. Sure thing! On the Columbia Wheel—that was the biggest time in them days.

(Sighs regretfully) But I'm retired now. I'm lettin' Patsie carry on the old traditions—

PATSIE. Now, Mom—

MRS. LINDEN. Well, it's nothin' to be ashamed of. It was a good, honest livin', anyway.

PATSIE. I know. But Aunt Sue is liable to get the impression I'm in burlesque, too.

MRS. LINDEN. Now, how could she get that impression when she oughta know perfectly well there ain't any burlesque no more—not to speak of, there ain't.

PATSIE. *(With hauteur)* I'm in cabarets, myself.

MRS. LINDEN. *(Nods proudly)* The last job she had was in one of the finest cabarets in Hoboken.

FURBER. *(Enters C. from L. with several pieces of luggage)* Beg pardon, Mrs. Hollis. Where shall I put these?

MRS. HOLLIS. Oh, better take them straight up to the second floor guest room, Furber. I'll show the ladies up later.

FURBER. Very good, ma'am. *(Starts off R.)*

MRS. LINDEN. And, Sonnie, be careful of that little—

FURBER. Yes, madame, I know—the little brown bag. It has a most delightful gurgle. *(Exits C. to R.)*

MRS. LINDEN. He catches on quick. Does he work for you regular, dearie, or did he come with the property?

PATSIE. Mom! He's the butler— Don't you know what a butler is?

MRS. LINDEN. Certainly I know what a butler is— I've seen enough movies in my day.

PATSIE. *(Shakes her head)* Ain't it awful, Aunt Sue? In spite of all the learning I give her, I can't get her to act refined.

MRS. HOLLIS. Well, I wouldn't worry about it. Tell me, how did you happen to meet Barry?

PATSIE. Oh, didn't he never tell you?

Mrs. Hollis. I don't think so. It wasn't another train window?

Patsie. Train window? I should say not! It was the most romantic thing ever—just like a book.

Mrs. Hollis. Really?

Patsie. I was in swimming, and I musta gc‘ over my depth, or something. I nearly drowned—and I woulda, too—if it hadn't been for Barry.

Mrs. Hollis. He saved you?

Patsie. He certainly did—I owe my whole life to him.

Mrs. Hollis. Well, how heroic!

Mrs. Linden. Wasn't it, dearie? Only I could never figure out how Patsie come so close to drownin'—seein' she swims like a fish—

Patsie. Mom! Could I help it if I got a sudden cramp?

Mrs. Hollis. Certainly not—it can happen to anyone.

Patsie. Sure! And since that day, we knew we was just meant for each other. I ain't never looked at another man, and Barry's never looked at another girl. (Mrs. Hollis *has a sudden coughing spell*) What did you say?

Mrs. Hollis. I didn't say anything. Just a little cold, you know.

Mrs. Linden. A cold? Say, I got just the thing for that, in my little brow—

Patsie. *(Cuts her off)* What I like about Barry is he's so intelligent, don't you think?

Mrs. Hollis. Well, I'd never noticed particularly.

Patsie. Oh, I think so. And I can tell, on account of I'm that way myself.

Mrs. Linden. *(Nods)* That's a fact. She almost went to college one time—

Mrs. Hollis. Did she?

MRS. LINDEN. But at the last minute, I decided to spend the dough on a mink coat instead.

MRS. HOLLIS. Well, that was a very close thing, wasn't it?

PATSIE. That's the trouble with me. I'm too intelligent. *(Sighs)* Men never seem to wanna just talk about books.

MRS. LINDEN. She spent the whole winter readin' that "Gone With the Wind"—

MRS. HOLLIS. Oh?

MRS. LINDEN. Yeah, and before that it was "Anthony Adverse." She certainly keeps up with all the best lit'richoor. Although I keep tellin' her it's just a waste of time. Who ever got anywhere readin' books?

PATSIE. I can't seem to break myself of the habit. It's just the way I am, I guess.

MRS. HOLLIS. I understand.

PATSIE. You read, Aunt Sue?

MRS. HOLLIS. Well— *(Smiles)* I can take it or leave it alone.

FURBER. *(Enters C. from R.)* The room is ready, Mrs. Hollis.

MRS. HOLLIS. *(Rises)* Wouldn't you like to go upstairs and wash up after your trip?

PATSIE. *(Rises)* Sure!

MRS. LINDEN. Just a minute now till I get my slipper on— *(Has a hard time pulling it on)* Ouch! I'd like to meet the guy who invented feet. *(Stands up)* Okay, let's go.

MRS. HOLLIS. This way. *(They follow her to arch. The TELEPHONE rings)* Answer that, will you, Furber?

FURBER. *(Crossing to desk)* Yes, ma'am.

MRS. LINDEN. *(Looking around in hall)* Some dump you got here, dearie—reminds me of Grand Central. *(They exeunt C. to R.)*

FURBER. *(Answering telephone)* Mrs. Hollis' resi-

dence— You wish to speak to Miss Ann Furber?—
I'm sorry, but I'm afraid that is not possible. If you
care to give me a message, I'll see that she gets it—
Ralph Sanders?—Oh, yes, Mr. Sanders. This is
Ann's father— Yes, she's spoken of you. She'll be
glad to know you're in town— Central Hotel?—
Very well, I'll have her call you there at once—
You're welcome, sir. Goodbye. *(Hangs up, crosses
and exits R.I.)*

BARRY. *(After a moment, enters C. from L. Tosses
his hat on console table. Looks around and calls)*
Hello! Where is everybody? *(Shrugs; comes down
into room.)*

MRS. HOLLIS. *(From off R.)* Is that you, Barry?
(Enters C. from R.)

BARRY. How's your headache, Aunt Sue?

MRS. HOLLIS. Never mind about that. I've got a
surprise for you—

BARRY. Surprise?

MRS. HOLLIS. Your visitors have come.

BARRY. *(His face lights up)* Gladys! Where is she?

MRS. HOLLIS. No, not Gladys—

BARRY. Huh?

MRS. HOLLIS. *(Looking off R.)* Sshh! Here she
comes now.

PATSIE. *(Enters C. from R.)* Barry! I thought I
heard your voice—

BARRY. *(A sickly expression on his face)* Patsie!

PATSIE. Yeah! Your little dream girl— (MRS.
HOLLIS *smothers a laugh.* BARRY *glares at her)*
Come to give you a big surprise. *(Coyly)* Is oo
s'p'ised to see oo 'ittle dweam girl?

BARRY. I'm surprised.

PATSIE. And is oo 'appy to see oo 'ittle dweam
girl?

BARRY. Oh, sure—sure, happy as a lark. But how
—I mean why—er—what are you doing here?

PATSIE. *(Angrily)* What am I doing here? Say,

you ain't tryin' to give me the run-around, are you?

BARRY. No, no! But—how did you happen to come?

PATSIE. You know very well how I happened to come. Your Aunt invited me—

BARRY. *What?*

MRS. HOLLIS. That's right, Barry—she has the letter with her.

BARRY. *(It begins to dawn on him)* Holy—! P-P-Patsie, let me see that letter—*please.*

PATSIE. Why?

BARRY. *(Excitedly)* Never mind why—never mind! Let me see it—quick.

PATSIE. *(Shrugs)* Okay! Here. *(Opens purse, takes it out and gives it to him.)*

BARRY. *(Looks it over quickly; groans)* The wrong one! They got mixed—that's what happened —they got mixed.

PATSIE. What are you talking about?

BARRY. And now—Gladys! Omigosh! What'll *she* think—?

PATSIE. Gladys? Say, what's going on here? What are you trying to pull on me—?

BARRY. Patsie, you—you'll have to go way—

PATSIE. *(Her eyes narrowing) Why* will I have to go way?

(MRS. HOLLIS *is enjoying all this immensely.)*

BARRY. Because—because— *(A sudden inspiration)* Because I'm married.

PATSIE. *(Her turn to be jolted)* You're—married?   *(WARN Curtain.)*

BARRY. Sure! Sure, I'm married. And my wife's awfully jealous. She'll kill you if she finds you here—

PATSIE. Who you married to?

BARRY. Who? Er—to my wife.

PATSIE. What's her name?

BARRY. Her name? Er—Pats—er—Glad—er—er— *(He can't think of one.)*

PATSIE. I don't believe it. You're making the whole thing up—

BARRY. No, I'm not. I'm married—honest I am—

PATSIE. You're making it up. You never told me before you was—

BARRY. It—it was a very sudden wedding. *(Smiles brightly.)*

PATSIE. If you are, where is she?

BARRY. Who?

PATSIE. Your wife.

BARRY. Where? Oh, she's—she's—she's— *(As JUNE enters c. from L.)* Here she is now! *(Rushes to her; throws his arms around her)* Hello, darling!

JUNE. *(Astounded)* Why, Barry!

BARRY. Hello, sweetheart!

JUNE. What's the—

BARRY. Hello, precious!

JUNE. Matter with—

BARRY. *(Shouts)* Hello, *wife!*

JUNE. Wife?

BARRY. Sure! I'm your husband! Remember—? Your husband!

JUNE. What's the matter with you? Have you gone cra—?

(BARRY *kisses her to shut her up.)*

QUICK CURTAIN

ACT TWO

THE TIME: *That same evening. About half an hour later.*

THE PLACE: *The same.*

AT RISE: BARRY *and* JUNE *are discovered.* JUNE *is seated on the divan.* BARRY *is pacing back and forth excitedly.*

BARRY. A fine sister!

JUNE. What could I do?

BARRY. I must say—can't even get a little co-operation from you when I need it most.

JUNE. If you were going to invent a crazy story like that, you should have let me know before.

BARRY. Did you *have* to tell her you were my sister? Couldn't you let her go on *thinking* you were my wife?

JUNE. She never thought so, anyway. She could see you were making it all up.

BARRY. A fine mess! *(Sighs despondently and slumps down in chair* L.*)* Now I never will get rid of her.

JUNE. Serves you right for getting mixed up with a person of her type.

BARRY. I couldn't let her drown, could I?

JUNE. *(Smiles)* Couldn't you?

BARRY. If I'd known when I saved her life she was going to keep throwing it at me ever after, I'd never have done it. Why are women all so unreasonable?

JUNE. Oh, I suppose you never gave her any encouragement at all, did you?

BARRY. Hardly any. I let her wear my frat pin—and told her I couldn't live without her—but I never imagined she'd *believe* me.

JUNE. Poor Aunt Sue—had to miss all the fun because of her headache.

BARRY. Oh, she didn't miss so much of it. You—both of you—seem to be getting an awful lot of enjoyment out of my tragedy.

JUNE. What's so tragic about it?

BARRY. *(Looks at her reproachfully)* How can you say that? You haven't *lived* enough to appreciate it, Sis. Gladys—the only girl I ever thought enough about to look at twice—

JUNE. *(A hollow laugh)* Ha, ha!

BARRY. *(Gives her a withering look)* And now I've probably lost her for good. *(Rises)* But I'm not going to give up without a battle. *(Crosses to arch.)*

JUNE. Where are you going?

BARRY. To find a telephone—going to try to get her on long distance.

JUNE. Can't you use this telephone?

BARRY. And have Patsie walk in and hear everything I say?

JUNE. From the way she started attacking that steak in there, her appetite 'll probably keep her busy for quite some time.

BARRY. *(Shakes his head)* Can't take a chance. My whole future life is at stake, Sis. See you later. *(Exits c. to L.)*

FURBER. *(After a moment, enters R.1)* Has Mrs. Hollis retired, Miss June?

JUNE. Yes, she has, Furber.

FURBER. I was wondering if she wished me to bring her some aspirins.

JUNE. She got a couple from the bathroom before she went to bed.

FURBER. Oh, very good, Miss. *(Turns to exit.)*

JUNE. Haven't they finished their dinner yet?

FURBER. Just finishing, Miss June.

JUNE. They'll be coming in here?

FURBER. Yes, Miss.

JUNE. Then I'll be going up to my room. *(Rises)* One session with the Lindens is plenty.

KATHLEEN. *(Enters R.I and stands in door)* Excuse me, Miss June. Could I have a word with you, Furber?

JUNE. That's all right, Kathleen. I was just going upstairs. *(Crosses and exits C. to R.)*

FURBER. What is it, Kathleen?

KATHLEEN. *(Closes door and comes into room)* 'Tis about tonight, that's what.

FURBER. Tonight? How do you mean?

KATHLEEN. Are you after forgetting 'twas to be my night off?

FURBER. Oh, that? I'm sorry, Kathleen—but unexpected guests, you know.

KATHLEEN. And *what* guests! How did the likes of them ever get invited to a respectable house like this?

FURBER. I'm sure I don't know. But after all, that's hardly our business, now is it?

KATHLEEN. Well, it's my business to have a night off once a week—and especially tonight.

FURBER. Why tonight so especially?

KATHLEEN. Because I had an engagement with my counsellor, if you must know—

FURBER. Counsellor?

KATHLEEN. Yes. Now don't be after repeating it but— *(Looks around, then whispers)* I think we've got a line on my Percival—

FURBER. Oh! Well, well! That's fine, isn't it?

KATHLEEN. 'Twon't be fine for him if ever I put my hands on him, bad cess to his soul.

FURBER. And you've got a line on him? *(She nods)* Where did they find him?

KATHLEEN. Well, now, 'tisn't exactly sure we are, but my counsellor's been in touch with a private detective company in New York, and they think—they *think,* mind you—it's my Percival in the flesh they've located.

FURBER. Good! I hope for your sake they're right, Kathleen.

KATHLEEN. Oh, *you* hope? And how is it do you think I feel—after four years—?

FURBER. Four years? Has it been that long?

KATHLEEN. *(Nods)* Four years! And I've said a prayer every night of that time. I've been prayin' the good Lord 'd let me get my fingers about his neck—for just one little minute. *(Makes a choking gesture with her two hands.)*

FURBER. *(Smiles)* I shouldn't like to be in Percival's boots.

KATHLEEN. Nor he won't like to be in his own boots, neither. Now what I want to know is this—if I call the counsellor and make a date for tomorrow afternoon, will that be suitable to you?

FURBER. *(Considers)* Yes, if you get back in time to make dinner.

KATHLEEN. I will.

FURBER. And if it turns out they *are* right about your young man, no running off to New York without giving notice.

KATHLEEN. Don't you worry yourself none about that—

MRS. LINDEN. *(Enters* R.I *with* PATSIE*)* That wasn't a bad little snack.

FURBER. I trust everything was satisfactory, madame.

Mrs. Linden. Well, I guess I've ate worse, Son-nie.

Furber. Thank you, madame. *(Bows.)*

Patsie. Whoo! I'm full up to here. *(Flops down on divan.* Mrs. Linden *sits with her.)*

Kathleen. I'll be after seein' about the dishes. *(Exits* R.I.*)*

Furber. Is there anything further you wish, madame?

Patsie. Where's Barry at?

Furber. I don't know, Miss. Shall I try to find him for you?

Patsie. Yeah. Tell him I wanna see him. Tell him me and him 've got plenty to talk over.

Furber. Very good, Miss. *(Exits* C. to R.*)*

Mrs. Linden. *(Kicks off her shoe)* They make these size seven shoes smaller every year.

Patsie. Say, Mom—you don't think he ran out on me, do you?

Mrs. Linden. Naw! Where would he run to? We're here, ain't we?

Patsie. The nerve of him! Trying to make me think he was married to his own sister. What do you s'pose he wanted to do that for?

Mrs. Linden. Aw, he's just funny. One of them eggsentric millionaires you read about in the papers.

Patsie. *(Sighs)* He don't seem awful anxious to get hitched up, does he?

Mrs. Linden. Don't worry—he will.

Patsie. How do you know?

Mrs. Linden. You still got those letters he sent you when we was at the beach?

Patsie. Yeah, I got 'em.

Mrs. Linden. Keep them. Them letters is as good as a wedding ring.

Patsie. *(Blankly)* Huh?

Mrs. Linden. *(Looks at her; shakes her head*

sadly) Your education is been sadly neglected—ain't you never heard of "breach of promise"?

PATSIE. Breach of promise? That wouldn't be ladylike, Mom.

MRS. LINDEN. Now lissen, Baby, it'll be time enough to think about ettyquette *after* you're married.

PATSIE. I know. Still in all, I wish we could do the whole thing refined. With a big church wedding, like all them swells have. And newsreels.

MRS. LINDEN. The main thing is not *how* but when—that's what I wanna find out.

PATSIE. I don't like the idea of breach of promise. It ain't bein' done in the best circles. *(Waxing indignant)* After all them vows he made to me and all. He'll either marry me refined, or I'll bop him one on the nose.

MRS. LINDEN. Now, Baby! You don't get nowhere getting excited—that's what we got courts for.

FURBER. *(Enters c. from R.)* I'm sorry, madame— Mr. Barry doesn't seem to be around.

PATSIE. Not around? Where'd he go to?

FURBER. I couldn't say, Miss. *(Crosses down R.)* He will undoubtedly return shortly. *(Exits R. I.)*

PATSIE. *(Alarmed)* Mom! Supposing he's taken a runout powder?

MRS. LINDEN. What's the diff, Baby? This is a comfortable house, the food's okay, and as far as I'm concerned, he don't never need to come back.

PATSIE. Yeah, but him runnin' out on me— What would all my friends in Hoboken say? And us a long way from home and all— *(Rises)* I gotta find him, Mom—

BARRY. *(Enters c. from L. He is carrying a "baby")* Hello!

PATSIE. *(Her jaw drops in amazement)* What—? *(She stares at him a moment)* Well, for Pete's sake, what've you got there?

BARRY. A—baby. Ha, ha—cute little thing, isn't it? *(Laughs nervously.)*

PATSIE. Where did you get it?

BARRY. Oh, it's—er—it's mine.

PATSIE. *(Shocked)* Yours?

MRS. LINDEN. *(Rises, incredulous, forgetting about her shoe)* Yours?

BARRY. Sure—ha, ha! *(A very forced laugh.)*

PATSIE. Lissen, Barry, what are you talking about?

MRS. LINDEN. Yeah, what's the big idea? What are you tryin' to pull on us—?

BARRY. *(With what he hopes is an innocent smile)* Haven't you heard of babies? People have them all the time, you know—

PATSIE. You mean to say you're its father?

BARRY. Sure!

PATSIE. And who's the mother?

(ANN *enters* R.I. *In the general excitement, the* OTHERS *don't notice her standing in the door.)*

BARRY. Er—my wife!

MRS. LINDEN. Are you tryin' to give us that again, Sonnie? You ain't got a wife—

BARRY. Oh—er—yes, I have—

PATSIE. Who—your sister?

BARRY. Yes, my—! No! No—er—someone else—

PATSIE. *(Insistently)* Who?

BARRY. Er—who?

MRS. LINDEN. Yeah, and where is she?

BARRY. Er—where is she?

PATSIE. And quit stalling. I bet you're making the whole thing up again—just like you did the last time.

BARRY. Oh, no! I—I could hardly make up the *baby*, could I?

MRS. LINDEN. I don't know. You eggsentric millionaires think you can get away with anything—

PATSIE. For the last time, if that's really your baby, who's the mother?

ANN. *(Quietly)* I am.

(Amazed, they ALL *whirl to face her.)*

MRS. LINDEN *and* PATSIE. *(Together)* You?

PATSIE. Who're you?

ANN. You'd better introduce me, Barry.

BARRY. Er—yes. This is—er—Ann.

PATSIE. Your wife?

BARRY. Er—no—I mean yes! Er—*are* you, Ann?

ANN. Certainly I am—don't be silly.

BARRY. Certainly she is—don't be silly.

ANN. And the mother of your baby.

BARRY. *(Nods his head to* OTHERS; *excitedly)* And the baby of my mother—er—the mother of my baby.

PATSIE. *(Vindictively to* ANN) You got no right to him. I saw him first.

ANN. Oh, no—I saw him long before you did, my dear.

MRS. LINDEN. If you're his wife, dearie, where you been keeping yourself all the time he was at Princeton?

ANN. Well, you see, I—why—I—

BARRY. *(Quickly)* She's been sick.

ANN. *(Relieved)* Yes—I've been sick.

PATSIE. Sick?

BARRY. Sure— *(Brightly)* Sleeping sickness!

MRS. LINDEN. Sleeping sickness? Oh, my gawd! *(Hobbles away from her in alarm.)*

PATSIE. Why didn't you never tell me about her?

BARRY. Well, I—I sort of—forgot—

PATSIE. Forgot? Forgot you had a wife?

BARRY. Uh-huh! My—my memory's terrible, you know—

MRS. LINDEN. Say, that sleeping sickness is catching, ain't it?

ANN. Oh, yes. It's practically always fatal— *(Smiles sweetly at her.)*

MRS. LINDEN. Oohh! Keep away from me—keep away, dearie. *(Backs as far away from her as she can get.)*

PATSIE. *(To* BARRY*)* And I suppose you forgot you had a baby, too?

BARRY. No, I—that is, you see—er—

ANN. *(Coming to his rescue)* He didn't know about it.

BARRY. No, I didn't know about it.

ANN. I've been keeping it from him—I wanted it to be a surprise.

PATSIE. What's the baby's name?

BARRY. Her name is Ann.⎱ *(Together)*
ANN. His name is Barry. ⎰

PATSIE. *(Suspiciously) What?*

BARRY. I mean—er—Ann Barry—

PATSIE. Ann Barry?

BARRY. *(A sudden inspiration)* Cran-berry.

ANN. *(Helping him out)* Uh-huh! Cranberry! And we call him "Berry-Berry" for short. Don't you think it's cute?

PATSIE. Personally, *I* think the whole thing is screwy. It don't make no sense at all. *(To* BARRY*)* *You* married a wife and forgot about her. *(To* ANN*)* And *you* had a baby but you didn't tell your husband because you wanted it to be a surprise. *(To* BOTH*)* And you named the baby Cranberry but you call him Berry-Berry for short. *(Shakes her head; sighs)* You got something there, pals, you got something.

MRS. LINDEN. Didn't I warn you? All million-aires is the same—batty as can be!

ANN. *(To ease the tension)* Let me have the little

darling, Barry. *(Takes the* BABY *from him)* Mother's little precious! Nice little Berry-Berry!

MRS. LINDEN. What are you doing? You wanna give him the sleeping sickness?

ANN. Oh, that's all right— *(Smiles reassuringly)* He's had it already.

MRS. LINDEN. *(Unbelievingly)* Him—sleeping sickness?

BARRY. Oh, sure—he got it while he was recovering from a slight attack of—er—leprosy.

PATSIE. How do you know so much about it, if you've never seen the kid till today?

ANN. I told him.

BARRY. Sure, she told me.

PATSIE. Is this on the level? Are you two really married, and is that really your kid?

ANN. Why, certainly! You don't think we'd *lie* to you, do you? *(The picture of injured innocence)* How could you think such a thing? *(Cooing to* BABY*)* Sweet little thing! Sweet little Berry-Berry!

BARRY. Er—uh—don't you think you'd better go, Patsie? I don't think the excitement is good for Ann —she's pretty weak. (ANN *coughs hollowly for his benefit)* See?

PATSIE. *(Sighs)* I suppose it's back to Hoboken for us.

MRS. LINDEN. *(Pokes her in the ribs; a stage whisper)* Breach of promise! Breach of promise!

PATSIE. No, Mom! It won't work. How can you sue a married man for breach of promise?

BARRY. *(Laughs self-consciously)* Yes, ha, ha! Silly to even think about it.

MRS. LINDEN. Well—a broken heart oughta be worth something—and you got a broken heart, ain't you, Baby?

PATSIE. *(Shakes her head)* I ain't gonna take him to court. It wouldn't be refined.

MRS. LINDEN. *(An expression of extreme disgust)*

Refined! Your manners 'll land us in the poorhouse yet, Baby!

PATSIE. We might as well start packing. *(Crosses to arch.)*

MRS. LINDEN. Okay! It's your funeral— *(Starts hobbling after her.)*

BARRY. Your shoe! *(Picks it up and hands it to her.)*

MRS. LINDEN. Oh, yeah—my shoe. *(Sits on divan to put it on.)*

MRS. HOLLIS. *(Enters C. from R. She is wearing a dressing gown and slippers)* Excuse me. I found I couldn't sleep after all and decided to have a cup of tea— *(Not paying much attention, she crosses down past them, opens door R.1 and calls)* Oh, Furber! *(Turns to them. They are regarding her very nervously)* Hello, Ann— *(As she sees the BABY)* Why—why, Ann! What's *that?*

ANN. *(Apprehensively)* Oh, that? It's—er—the baby, *Aunt Sue.*

BARRY. Yeah, the *baby*, Aunt Sue.

FURBER. *(Enters R.1)* Did you wish something, Mrs.— *(Horrified, as he takes in ANN and the BABY)* Mrs.—Mrs.— *(Unable to control himself)* Ann!

ANN. Aren't you forgetting yourself, *Furber? (A fierce whisper to BARRY)* Here! Take it! *(Thrusts BABY into his hands.)*

FURBER. *(Looking from one to the other)* Why, Mr. Barry! Ann!

ANN. *Miss* Ann to you, Furber! I mean, *Mrs.* Ann! I mean— *(Trails off lamely.)*

BARRY. *(Trying to explain to LINDENS)* Ha, ha! Furber's been with us a long time. He's a little familiar—

PATSIE. Yeah—just a little.

MRS. LINDEN. *(Having difficulty with the shoe)* This blamed slipper!

BARRY. Let me give you a hand with it, Mrs. Linden— *(Hands the* BABY *to* MRS. HOLLIS*)* Here, Aunt Sue—

MRS. HOLLIS. Why—what is it?

BARRY. You know, Aunt Sue—it's your—grand-child.

MRS. HOLLIS. *Grandchild?*

BARRY. I mean—your niece!

MRS. HOLLIS. Niece—?

BARRY. Yes, your *niece*, Aunt Sue! *(Kicks her in the shin. She jumps)* Remember?

MRS. HOLLIS. Oh! Yes—my niece! Of course! *(Uncertainly to* BABY*)* Hello, niece— Have you been a good girl?

BARRY. *(Quickly, as he realizes his error)* I mean —your *nephew!* Little Cranberry!

MRS. HOLLIS. *(Dazedly)* Yes, my nephew—little Cranberry—

BARRY. *(To* LINDENS*)* Ha, ha! All the Hollises have bad memories— *(Quickly as he looks at* MRS. HOLLIS*)* Even the Hollises by marriage!

MRS. LINDEN. *(Finally succeeding in getting her shoe on)* There! I guess I'm ready.

PATSIE. Then let's get out of here before we go cuckoo, too.

MRS. LINDEN. You said it, Baby! *(They exeunt* C. *to* R.*)*

MRS. HOLLIS. Barry! Will you kindly tell me—?

FURBER. *(Simultaneously with* MRS. HOLLIS*)* Ann! What is the meaning—?

BARRY. *(Frantically)* Sshh! Sshh! *(Crosses to arch; looks off to make sure they're gone)* Whoo! *(Slumps down in chair up* L. *and mops his brow)* What a night! What a night!

MRS. HOLLIS. *(Crosses to him)* Barry! I presume there *is* an explanation of all this?

BARRY. *(Wearily)* What?

MRS. HOLLIS. Where did you get this—this little person?

BARRY. Oh, I— *(Carelessly, with a wave of the hand)* Just picked it up.

MRS. HOLLIS. Just picked it up?

BARRY. Yeah. I had to get them—out of the house some way. And I was walking along and saw this baby sleeping on a porch, and I thought that would do the trick—so I just picked it up.

MRS. HOLLIS. Good heavens!

BARRY. And it worked—they're leaving. But, boy —what a job!

FURBER. Then, Ann—it's *not* yours—I mean—you didn't have anything to do with—I mean—

ANN. Why, Father! Certainly not! *(Laughs)* What an idea! I was just helping Barry out—

FURBER. Er—helping him out?

ANN. Uh-huh! When he told them the baby was his, they insisted on seeing its mother, so I— *(Airily)* just thought I'd give him a hand.

FURBER. Yes. To be sure.

BARRY. You saved my life, Ann.

ANN. Oh, it was nothing. Glad to be your wife any time. Just call on me.

MRS. HOLLIS. But, Barry, you picked the baby up without telling its parents? What will they think?

BARRY. I'll have it back before they know anything about it. Just as soon as our dear guests go.

MRS. HOLLIS. Here! Take it! *(Thrusts the BABY into his hands)* My grandchild! Little "Gooseberry," indeed!

BARRY. *(Grins) Cran*-berry, Aunt Sue!

MRS. HOLLIS. And you were going to be as industrious as a beaver—

BARRY. I have been tonight, haven't I?

MRS. HOLLIS. *(Smiles sardonically at him)* I can't remember ever hearing of a beaver with a baby named Cranberry. *(Crossing to* R.I) Well, come along, Furber, and fix me a pot of tea.

FURBER. Very good, ma'am.

MRS. HOLLIS. At any rate, life with the Hollises is anything but humdrum, now that Barry is back. *(Exits* R.I.)

FURBER. Ann, don't you think—?

ANN. I'll be right along, Father.

FURBER. Er—yes. *(Looks from one to the other significantly)* Yes, my dear. *(Exits* R.I.)

BARRY. *(Looking at the* BABY) Cute little cuss, isn't he?

ANN. *(Crosses to him; looks down at* BABY; *smiles)* Uh-huh! I wonder what its name really is.

BARRY. Oh, Johnnie, probably. Most babies are named Johnnie.

ANN. Are you sure it's that kind of a baby? Maybe it's a Mary.

BARRY. Either way, it'll always be Cranberry to me.

ANN. Me, too! Berry-Berry for short!

BARRY. Babies are wonderful things, aren't they? He's been sleeping sound as a top all through everything.

ANN. Maybe he feels he's in good hands.

BARRY. You've been a big help to me tonight, Ann. I don't know how I can ever thank you.

ANN. Oh, you don't have to. It was fun.

BARRY. You understand how I feel about Patsie and her mother. I guess it was all my fault—getting mixed up with her in the first place—but—

ANN. Oh, that's quite all right, Barry. Don't feel you have to explain to *me*.

BARRY. No, I don't, but—I just wanted you to know. I'm doing it all for— *(Sighs longingly)* Gladys!

ANN. *(Her face falls)* Gladys?

BARRY. A girl I met on the train. You'd love her,

Ann. She's the most adorable—the most charming —the most—you'd love her.

ANN. I'm sure I would.

BARRY. I hope you'll have the pleasure of meeting her soon.

ANN. I hope so.

BARRY. I'm sort of in a little hot water with her already. Tried to get her on the phone a little while ago, but there wasn't any answer.

ANN. Well—I'm sure I wish you all the luck in the world.

BARRY. Thanks— *(Looks at* BABY*)* Hey! He's waking up. What'll I do?

ANN. Why not sing him a lullaby?

BARRY. Good idea! *(Rises, walks around, rocking the* BABY *in his arms and singing)* "La, la, la, la, la— On the tree top! La, la, la, la—the cradle will rock!"

(DOORBELL rings.)

ANN. Isn't that the bell?

BARRY. Sshh! I think he's falling asleep again— *(Sings)* "La, la, la, la, la—"

FURBER. *(Enters* R.1*)* Pardon me, sir. *(Crosses and exits* C. *to* L.*)*

BARRY. "When the bough breaks— La, la, la, la, la—" Atta kid, Berry-Berry! Go to sleep— Close your eyes—

FURBER. *(Re-enters* C. *from* L.*)* Miss Gladys Vance to see you, Mr. Barry—

BARRY. That's right—close your— *(As it sinks in) Wha-a-at?* Gladys—here—? Omigosh! *(Excitedly starts to rush out arch. Comes rushing back; thrusts* BABY *upon* ANN*)* Here! You take care of him, Ann.

ANN. But—

BARRY. Be a good sport— *(Looks around frantically)* Wait in there! *(Rushes her to* R.2 *and opens door.)*

ANN. All right! *(Exits* R.2.*)*

BARRY. Well, what are you waiting for, Furber? Show her in—show her in!

FURBER. Very good, sir. *(Exits* C. *to* L.*)*

GLADYS. *(Enters* C. *from* L., *followed by* FURBER. *Latter is carrying an overnight bag)* Hello, Barry!

BARRY. Gladys! Well, for—! Gosh! I'm glad to—! Gladys! *(Speechlessly happy.)*

FURBER. Beg pardon, Mr. Barry— *(Indicates overnight bag)* What shall I do with this, sir?

BARRY. Oh, just leave it there for the time being.

FURBER. Very good, sir. *(Puts bag on console table and crosses down* R.*)*

BARRY. *(Excitedly to* GLADYS*)* Will you have something to eat—? Will you have something to drink—? Will you have *something?*

GLADYS. No, thanks.

BARRY. That's all. Furber.

FURBER. Yes, sir. *(Exits* R.I.*)*

BARRY. It's good to see you, Gladys—it's *swell* to see you—

GLADYS. I'm annoyed.

BARRY. *(Nervously)* I know—I know. It was all a mistake—believe me—just a mistake. *(Takes her arm)* Let's sit down and I'll tell you all about it.

GLADYS. All right! *(He leads her to divan and they sit.)*

BARRY. I know what you're annoyed about. You got a note telling you not to come, didn't you?

GLADYS. I did. And you called me "Patsie," when you know perfectly well my name is Gladys.

BARRY. No, no! You don't understand—the notes got mixed. The note I really intended for you was an invitation—a very *warm* invitation.

GLADYS. I thought there must have been some mistake. I thought, from the way you talked on the train, you really *wanted* me to come—

BARRY. Certainly! *(Smiles brightly)* Just a mistake! But let's not talk about that. Now you're here, and—

GLADYS. But who *is* Patsie—?

BARRY. Patsie? Oh, she's—er—my grandmother.

GLADYS. Your grandmother?

BARRY. Yes. We—we always call her Patsie, you know—

GLADYS. Why?

BARRY. Why? Oh—er—because that's her name. Don't you think it's cute?

GLADYS. If Patsie's your grandmother, what was she doing with your frat pin?

BARRY. Oh, that's easy. She—she wanted it for my grandfather.

GLADYS. For your grandfather?

BARRY. Yes. He was thinking of joining a fraternity, and she wanted him to have it—

GLADYS. Then why did you ask her to send it back?

BARRY. Because—because he decided to join the Elks instead. See?

GLADYS. *(Looks very doubtful)* H'mm! Your grandfather wanted to join a fraternity, did he?

BARRY. Anyway, that's settled. You're here, and that's all that matters.

GLADYS. *(After slight pause)* Is it?

BARRY. You've been on my mind ever since I met you on the train.

GLADYS. *(Smiles gayly)* I've thought of you lots, too.

BARRY. *(Tickled) Really?*

GLADYS. Really!

BARRY. Gosh! *(Sighs happily. Snuggles up to her)* Gladys—do you believe in love at first sight?

GLADYS. *(Coquettishly)* I don't know. Do *you?*

BARRY. Certainly! I've always said, when the right girl came along, I'd know it just like that—- *(Snaps his fingers.)*

GLADYS. And has she come along?

BARRY. *(Looking intently into her eyes)* Yes!

GLADYS. *(Looking away, shyly)* Oh, Barry!

BARRY. I knew it the minute I saw you, Gladys. You said, "Will you open my window for me, please?" And I said to myself, "Barry, there she is."

GLADYS. Just like that?

BARRY. Just like that. *(Fervently)* And since that moment, Gladys, I haven't *looked* at another girl. I haven't looked at one for so much as a split second—

PATSIE. *(Enters c. from R., followed by* MRS. LINDEN*)* We're packed, Barry—

BARRY. *(Jumps to his feet; very nervously)* Oh— are you?

PATSIE. *(Eyes* GLADYS *interestedly; comes into room)* Well, who's the girl friend?

BARRY. *(Trying to appear casual)* Oh—just some girl I met on a train.

PATSIE. Well, ain't you gonna introduce us?

BARRY. Er—um—aren't you in a hurry?

MRS. LINDEN. We can wait.

PATSIE. Sure, we can wait.

BARRY. *(As they* ALL *cross down to divan)* This is Gladys Vance—

GLADYS. How do you do?

BARRY. And this is Mrs. Linden, and Pats— *(Quickly, remembering his "grandmother")* I mean *Miss* Linden!

PATSIE. Hiyah!

BARRY. *(Very worried)* Mrs. Linden and Miss Linden were just leaving, weren't you?

PATSIE. Yeah, we were—

BARRY. *(Trying to get them up to arch)* Well, don't let us delay you. Come on, I'll show you the way out—

MRS. LINDEN. We might as well go, Patsie.

GLADYS. *(Suspiciously)* Is your name Patsie, Miss Linden?

PATSIE. Sure! What's it to you?

GLADYS. Oh, nothing.

BARRY. *(Laughs nervously)* Ha, ha! She's got the same name as my grandmother. Isn't that a coincidence?

GLADYS. It certainly is!

PATSIE. Before we leave, Barry, we'd better say goodbye to your wife— (GLADYS *rises, horrified)* and kid.

GLADYS. Barry!

BARRY. *(Tongue-tied with terror)* My—er—er—er— What did you say?

MRS. LINDEN. She said your wife and ba—

BARRY. *(Quickly)* I heard her.

PATSIE. Well, where are they?

BARRY. *(Looks helplessly from PATSIE to GLADYS)* They—aren't.

PATSIE. *What?*

BARRY. I mean—they aren't here. They—they're gone.

GLADYS. *(Turns away from him, revolted)* Oh, Barry!

BARRY. *(Miserably)* Gladys—please! I can explain—

MRS. LINDEN. He certainly can, dearie. He's one of the best little explainers you ever saw—

ANN. *(Enters R.2 with the BABY)* Did I hear someone calling for me?

PATSIE. We was just leaving, Mrs. Hollis. We wanted to say goodbye.

ANN. Oh! *(Crosses to BARRY and links an arm in his)* Well, come back and see us again soon. I know dear little Berry-Berry just loves having you.

(BARRY *stands there looking limp with worry.)*

PATSIE. Thanks. I guess we'll have to call a cab—

BARRY. I'll call it for you. *(Crosses to desk; dials a number. In telephone)* Hello— Send a cab to the Hollis house— That's right— Martin Drive— And make it quick. *(Hangs up.)*

GLADYS. I'll go, too— *(Starts for arch.)*

BARRY. *(Grabs her arm)* Don't! Not yet—Gladys! I want to talk to you—

GLADYS. Well, I don't want to talk to *you*— *(Tries to pull away from him.)*

BARRY. *Please!*

GLADYS. Let go of me. What will your wife think?

ANN. *(Smiles brightly)* Oh, I don't mind—I'm used to it.

BARRY. *(Still holding on to* GLADYS, *who is trying to break out of his hold. To* PATSIE*)* Why don't you wait out in the hall? It's—it's quicker.

PATSIE. *(Shrugs)* Come on, Mom. I guess we can take a hint.

MRS. LINDEN. *(Disgusted)* You'll be refined if it kills you. *(They exeunt* C. *to* L.*)*

GLADYS. Let go of me, you—you bigamist!

BARRY. Gladys! Listen to reason—

GLADYS. I want to get out of here—I'm not safe in this house.

BARRY. But I'm *not* married. It's you I love.

GLADYS. *(Calms down a little)* What? You're *not* married?

BARRY. No! Absolutely not!

GLADYS. I don't believe it.

BARRY. You tell her, Ann.

ANN. He *isn't* married, and it *is* you he loves.

GLADYS. But I—I don't understand. Those other women—?

BARRY. They *think* I'm married. I had to tell them that because they were going to sue me for breach of promise.

ANN. What did you promise them?

BARRY. Oh—nothing.

ANN. I see. They were going to sue you for promising them nothing.

BARRY. (Groans) It's so complicated. But they're leaving now, and everything's going to be hunky-dory. You've *got* to believe me, Gladys—you've *got* to trust me.

GLADYS. (Nods toward ANN) If she's not your wife, who is she?

BARRY. Ann.

GLADYS. Ann?

ANN. Just Ann. I've been helping Barry out. He needed a wife in a hurry, so I was it.

GLADYS. And the baby?

BARRY. Berry-Berry? I borrowed him—sort of. To make Patsie believe I'm really married to Ann—

ANNE. Which he's not.

BARRY. Which I'm not.

GLADYS. Patsie! She's rather young for a grand-mother, don't you think?

BARRY. It was all a mistake, Gladys—*honestly.* (Savagely) Those confounded notes! But that's all in the past. Believe me, I'll be a different man from now on.

GLADYS. You're sure you're not married—to *any-one?*

BARRY. Sure!

GLADYS. That's *not* your baby?

BARRY. No!

GLADYS. And you *do* want me to stay?

BARRY. Yes!

GLADYS. (Little pause) I'll stay. (Comes down and sits in divan.)

BARRY. Good! And please, Gladys—please try to forget everything you've seen tonight. Pretend it didn't happen and—

ANN. *(Looking at* BABY*)* Barry!

BARRY. What's the matter now?

ANN. Berry-Berry—he's waking up again.

BARRY. Well, sing to him—like I did. That'll keep him quiet.

ANN. *(Crooning)* "La, la, la, la, la—!"

(DOORBELL rings.)

BARRY. That must be their cab.

FURBER. *(Enters* R.1*)* Pardon me, please. *(Crosses and exits* C. *to* L.*)*

ANN. "La, la, la, la, la! When the wind blows—La, la, la, la, la—!"

RALPH. *(In a loud voice, from off up* L.*)* I've got to see her, I tell you. Let me in. *(Enters* C. *from* L., *pushing* FURBER *in front of him. They are followed by* PATSIE *and* MRS. LINDEN, *who stand watching curiously.)*

ANN. *(Astonished)* Ralph! Ralph Sanders! What are you doing here?

RALPH. I had to see you, Ann. You didn't call me, and I've been worried sick— *(Breaks off as he sees* BABY*)* What are you doing with that baby?

ANN. Oh, I—I'm just minding it for someone—

PATSIE. Huh? What's that?

BARRY. *(Under his breath to* ANN*)* Ixnay! *(To* RALPH*)* It's hers—ours—Ann's and mine!

RALPH. *(Belligerently)* Who're you?

BARRY. I'm Barry Hollis, and this is my house. Who're you?

ANN. Oh, I'm sorry. This is Ralph Sanders, Barry—a—a friend from New York.

RALPH. What's this fellow to you, Ann?

BARRY. She's my wife.

RALPH. Ann! Is this true?

ANN. *(Helplessly)* Well—I— Yes!

(BARRY nods, relieved.)

RALPH. You've been married to him all the time—
all the time you led me to believe you cared for me?

ANN. *(Slight pause)* Yes!

RALPH. *(Bitterly)* Ann! How could you?

ANN. I—I'm sorry.

RALPH. *(Laughs cynically)* Oh, you're sorry!
Well, I warned you, Ann. I told you what I'd do if
you turned me down—

ANN. *(Alarmed)* Ralph—wait.

RALPH. I warned you—and I'm going to do it.
(Whips out a revolver.)

(Exclamations of consternation from ALL.)

ANN. Ralph! Don't! Don't!

RALPH. I said I wouldn't let anybody come between us—and I won't. *(Points revolver at BARRY.)*

ANN. What are you going to do?

RALPH. *(Snarls)* I'm going to kill him.

BARRY. S-s-see here, old man—y-y-you can't do
that.

RALPH. Why can't I?

BARRY. B-b-because—because—it would be rather
messy, you know— *(Laughs nervously)* Ha, ha, ha!

RALPH. Shut up and say your prayers.

BARRY. M-m-must I?

RALPH. Yes! You stole the woman I love, and
now you're going to pay for it.

BARRY. *(Desperately)* B-b-but I didn't steal her.
She—she's not my wife. We're—we're not married
at all.

PATSIE. Not married?

RALPH. What's this? What's this?

ANN. It's true, Ralph. We only pretended to be
married because—because these women were going
to sue him for breach of promise—

PATSIE. Well, how do you like that! And I trusted him—I trusted him implicitly—like a perfect lady.

MRS. LINDEN. See, Baby? I told you that refinement stuff don't get you nowhere—

RALPH. *(To* BARRY*)* Is this on the level?

BARRY. Yes! Honest! P-p-put that gun down, will you, old man?

RALPH. You're not just saying it because you don't want me to shoot you?

BARRY. No! It's the truth, the whole truth, and nothing but the truth, so help me.

(DOORBELL rings.)

FURBER. Pardon me, sir—

RALPH. Stay where you are.

FURBER. But the doorbell—it's ringing—

RALPH. Let it ring. I've got to get this straight first.

FURBER. Er—very good, sir.

(DOORBELL continues to ring insistently.)

RALPH. If I don't shoot him, Ann, will you promise to marry me?

ANN. Yes!

RALPH. At once? Immediately?

ANN. Yes, yes! Only don't shoot him—

PATSIE. *(Indignantly)* Let me have that gun and I'll shoot him myself.

MRS. JONES. *(From off up* L.*)* I know there's somebody here and I'm coming in. *(Enters* C. *from* L.*)*

FURBER. *(Intercepting her in arch)* Beg pardon, madame. Did you wish to see someone?

MRS. JONES. Darn right, I did!

FURBER. What name, please?

MRS. JONES. The name is Jones, and I'm looking for my baby.

ANN. Good heavens! Here! *(Thrusts the* BABY *into* BARRY'S *hands. He stands holding it and looking as though he'd like to sink through the floor.)*

FURBER. Isn't there some mistake, madame?

MRS. JONES. No, there's no mistake. The boy said he saw a man coming into this house with my baby, and I want her.

FURBER. Er—there's no baby here, madame—

PATSIE. Oh, yes, there is.

(WARN Curtain.)

MRS. JONES. Where? *(Whirls around to her.)*

PATSIE. There! *(Points to* BARRY, *who has been trying to shield the* BABY *from* MRS. JONES'S *sight.)*

MRS. JONES. *(Rushes over to him; takes one look at the* BABY*)* Gwendolyn! *(Tears it from his arms.)*

BARRY. Gwendolyn? Er—that's a nice name, isn't it?

MRS. JONES. *(Almost hysterical with joy)* Gwendolyn! Kutchy-wutchy-kutchy! Kutchy-wutchy-kutchy!

BARRY. You'll find Gwendolyn practically as good as new—

MRS. JONES. Kutchy-wutchy-kutchy! Kutchy-wutchy-kutchy! Is Mama's little darling all right?

BARRY. Oh, yes—perfectly all right!

MRS. JONES. *(The* BABY *clutched tightly to her breast, she advances menacingly on* BARRY*)* You—! You—!

BARRY. *(Backing away)* Listen—I can explain everything—I only borrowed it—

MRS. JONES. *Borrowed* it? Borrowed my baby—?

BARRY. Uh-huh! Just for a little while—I was going to give it back—

MRS. JONES. You *stole* her.

BARRY. No, no!

MRS. JONES. You stole her. You stole my little

kutchy-wutchy. But there's laws to protect people from vipers like you. I'll go to the police. I'll have you arrested. I'll have you sent up for life. I'll have you electrocuted. You—you—you *kidnaper!*

QUICK CURTAIN

ACT THREE

THE TIME: *That same night. About two hours later.*

THE PLACE: *The same.*

AT RISE: GLADYS, PATSIE *and* MRS. LINDEN *are on the divan.* PATSIE *and* MRS. LINDEN *are both leaning back, sound asleep.* GLADYS *is trying to read a book.* JUNE *is seated up* L., ANN *down* L. *and* RALPH *at the desk.* MRS. HOLLIS, *looking very worried, is in the chair down* R. *A moment or two after the Curtain rises,* MRS. LINDEN *gives a particularly loud snore, and this wakes up* PATSIE.

PATSIE. *(Looking up sleepily. Pokes* MRS. LINDEN*)* Hey, Mom! Mom!
MRS. LINDEN. *(Awakes with a start)* Huh? Whatsa matter?
PATSIE. You been snoring—
MRS. LINDEN. Have I?
PATSIE. What'll everyone think?
MRS. LINDEN. I can't help what they think. When I sleep, I snore, and I'm sleepy.
PATSIE. *(To* MRS. HOLLIS*)* Ain't he back yet?
MRS. HOLLIS. *(Sighs ruefully)* Not yet.
PATSIE. He's still in jail?
MRS. HOLLIS. Yes.
PATSIE. I thought you said that lawyer was good?

63

MRS. HOLLIS. Mr. Miller will get him out—in time. He's very able.

MRS. LINDEN. Is he able on breach of promise suits, dearie? 'Cause your precious Barry's gonna have one on his hands if he ever gets outa *this* mess—

PATSIE. Now, Mom—

MRS. LINDEN. *(Flaring)* And don't tell me to act refined, or I'll crown ya one. What's all your refinement done for you so far—?

PATSIE. But—

MRS. LINDEN. *(Topping her)* Don't bother! I'll tell you: it's almost done you outa about three million dollars—that's what.

JUNE. *(Brightly)* The penalty for kidnaping in this state is twenty years to life—did you know that?

MRS. HOLLIS. *(Shudders)* June! Must you remind us of it?

ANN. Of course, it wasn't *really* kidnaping—everyone knows that.

GLADYS. But judges can be very funny about those things.

ANN. *(Sweetly)* How do you know about judges, Gladys?

GLADYS. *(Glares at her)* Only what I read in the papers, dear.

PATSIE. *(To GLADYS)* No use your hanging around, Sister. You might as well go home. Barry's gonna marry me.

GLADYS. Perhaps we'd better wait and let him decide for himself.

MRS. LINDEN. He ain't got nothin' to do with it. He's gonna marry Patsie—or else!

GLADYS. That remains to be seen.

MRS. LINDEN. No, it don't. Nothing remains to be seen. 'Cause from now on I'm forgetting my etty-quette and taking charge of things personally.

JUNE. *(Giggles)* Barry'll just love that.

MRS. HOLLIS. Quiet, June! Please—can't we talk about something else?

PATSIE. That's a good idea. *(Brightly)* Has anybody read "How To Win Friends and Influence People"? *(This remark is greeted by a stony silence)* No? *(Sighs)* I guess I'm the only one in the crowd interested in real litrichoor.

RALPH. *(After a slight pause)* Don't see what good *we're* doing, sticking around here, Ann.

ANN. I want to see how Barry makes out.

RALPH. Why? What's it mean to you?

ANN. I'm—interested. Naturally. You wouldn't want to see him go to prison, would you?

RALPH. I can't say it woula break my heart.

ANN. You can go if you want to—I'm staying here a while.

RALPH. Oh, no! If you stay—I stay, too. *(Breaks into a whistle; takes out his revolver and begins wiping it off with a handkerchief.)*

MRS. HOLLIS. Mr. Sanders! Would you mind putting that horrid thing away?

RALPH. Now, don't worry—I know how to handle one of these things. *You're* safe enough.

JUNE. *(Yawns)* Ho-hum! *(Rises)* I think I'll go up to bed.

MRS. HOLLIS. All right, dear.

JUNE. If there's any more excitement, call me, Aunt Sue.

MRS. HOLLIS. I hope there won't be.

JUNE. *(Crossing to arch)* Goodnight, folks. And— *(Smiles)* don't do anything I wouldn't do. *(Exits c. to R.)*

ANN. *(Rises; crosses to window; stands there a moment looking out)* Mr. Miller doesn't seem to be having such an easy time of it.

RALPH. Relax, Ann! Don't take it so hard.

ANN. Me? *(Trying to appear casual)* Why, I'm

not taking it hard at all. Oh, Mrs. Hollis, I hope you don't mind my—my staying around this way.

MRS. HOLLIS. Certainly not, Ann. You know you're always welcome.

ANN. The fact is—I feel sort of responsible—in a way, for everything that's happened tonight.

MRS. HOLLIS. Nonsense, my dear! Whatever's happened—I'm sure Barry brought it on himself.

PATSIE. Yeah, and a lot more that ain't happened —yet.

MRS. HOLLIS. *(Ignoring this)* At any rate, you mustn't feel you're ever in the way, Ann.

GLADYS. You're very informal here, aren't you, Mrs. Hollis? *(Cattily)* I mean I think it's so *democratic* of you, the way you seem to mix with the servants—

(ANN *whirls angrily; starts to say something.)*

MRS. HOLLIS. *(Quickly)* I find them much preferable to some other people, my dear Miss Vance.

(GLADYS *bites her lip.)*

MRS. LINDEN. *(Puzzled; to* PATSIE*)* What are they talking about, Baby?

PATSIE. They're saying how much they like each other.

MRS. LINDEN. Yeah?

PATSIE. That's the way they do it in society, Mom.

MRS. LINDEN. Well, I wish your boy friend would hurry up and get here, so you could get married and get away from this joint. I don't feel comfortable here.

MRS. HOLLIS. Is there something I could have Furber get for you, Mrs. Linden?

MRS. LINDEN. Well— *(Looks at* PATSIE; *holds up two fingers)* Maybe about this much of something to warm me— (PATSIE *pokes her; she pouts*) Aw, there you go again!

FURBER. *(Enters* R.I) I beg your pardon, Mrs. Hollis—

MRS. HOLLIS. Yes, what is it, Furber?

FURBER. I wish to speak to Ann. Can you spare her, ma'am?

MRS. HOLLIS. Why, of course.

ANN. Me, Father?

FURBER. Yes, my dear. Will you come with me, please?

ANN. What's it all about? *(Crosses to him.)*

RALPH. *(Rises; saunters over to them)* Maybe I'd better go along, too.

FURBER. You, sir?

RALPH. Sure! We might as well get to know each other. After all, you're going to be my father-in-law.

FURBER. Er—very good, Mr. Sanders As you wish, sir. This way, please. *(Holds the door open for them, and* RALPH *and* ANN *exeunt* R.I) Thank you, Mrs. Hollis. *(Exits after them.)*

MRS. HOLLIS. Wouldn't you like to go to your room, Miss Vance?

GLADYS. Thanks, no. I believe I'll wait for Barry, if you don't mind.

PATSIE. *(As* MRS. HOLLIS *glances at her)* Don't look at me—I'm sticking right here.

MRS. HOLLIS. Very well.

PATSIE. You can go up if you wanna, Mom.

MRS. LINDEN. Nothin' doing! I'm staying here and looking after you. I ain't trusting my whole future to a girl who thinks of nothing but ettyquette.

(DOORBELL rings.)

MRS. HOLLIS. Barry!

PATSIE. *(Jumps up quickly)* I'll let him in. *(Rushes off* C. *to* L.)

Mrs. Hollis. *(Rises; calls)* Never mind, Furber.

Patsie. *(Re-enters)* It's the lawyer.

Miller. *(Enters c. from l.)* Good evening!

Mrs. Hollis. Good heavens, Seth! You didn't get him off.

Miller. Yes, yes! Calm yourself, Sue. He'll be along directly. The desk sergeant is checking him out now.

Mrs. Hollis. He's free?

Miller. Yes. After a good deal of explaining, I managed to get him off with a reprimand.

Mrs. Hollis. Well, that's a relief.

Patsie. Yeah, good news, huh, Mom?

Mrs. Linden. Maybe he won't think so, after I get through having a little talk with him.

Miller. *(Looks inquiringly at* Others*)* Er—?

Mrs. Hollis. Forgive me! This is Mr. Miller—Barry's lawyer. Mrs. Linden—Miss Linden—and Miss Vance.

Miller. How do you do—how do you do?

(The Others *nod acknowledgment.)*

Mrs. Linden. You any good at breach of promise, Sonnie?

Miller. Er—breach of promise?

Mrs. Linden. *(Nods)* If you ain't you'd better start looking up the law books right now.

Miller. I do not understand.

Mrs. Linden. Never mind—you will.

Mrs. Hollis. *(Holds a hand to her head)* My headache—it seems to be returning.

Miller. I'm sorry, Sue. Can I get you something?

Mrs. Hollis. No, thanks, Seth. I believe I'll go back to bed. You won't need me any more, will you?

Miller. Well— *(Hesitates)* I have some—er—some very grave news for Barry.

MRS. HOLLIIS. Grave news? Good heavens! What is it?

MILLER. I prefer to wait until he gets here.

MRS. HOLLIS. It doesn't concern me?

MILLER. Er—only indirectly.

MRS. HOLLIS. In that case, I'll let him tell me about it in the morning. I've had enough "grave news" for one night.

MILLER. As you wish.

MRS. HOLLIS. *(Crosses to arch)* Goodnight, everybody! *(Smiles mischievously)* I do hope everything works out satisfactorily for all of you— *(Winces)* My head! Goodnight! *(Exits C. to R.)*

MILLER. *(Takes out his watch and looks at it; frowns)* H'mn! *(Sits down R.)*

PATSIE. Looks like we gotta do a little more waiting. *(Sits down L.)*

MILLER. *(To make conversation)* Er—pleasant evening, eh?

MRS. LINDEN. *(Looks at him coldly)* What's pleasant about it?

MILLER. Eh? Oh, nothing, nothing.

PATSIE. Didn't Barry give you no message for me?

MILLER. Oh, yes. He said he wanted you to wait here for him—all of you.

MRS. LINDEN. *(Sarcastically)* Now ain't that nice of him?

MILLER. Er—Mrs. Linden, what did you mean by that reference to breach of promise?

MRS. LINDEN. I meant Barry's gotta do one thing —and if he don't do it, he's gonna have a whale of a lawsuit on his hands.

MILLER. Lawsuit?

GLADYS. This person actually expects Barry to marry her, Mr. Miller. Isn't it too ridiculous?

PATSIE. *(Angrily)* This person'll crown you one on the beezer if you don't hold your tongue.

MRS. LINDEN. That's right, Baby—give her Hail Columbia. I think she's trying to cop your boy friend —that's what I think.

GLADYS. *(Her nose in the air)* Really, I don't care to discuss it with you.

MILLER. Oh, breach of promise, eh? *(Smiles)* That's quite funny.

MRS. LINDEN. What do you mean, it's funny?

MILLER. I don't think you'll sue Barry at all.

PATSIE. What's gonna stop us?

MILLER. *(Smiling to himself)* You'll see—you'll see.

BARRY. *(Comes rushing in* C. *from* L.) Hello!

GLADYS. *(As she and* PATSIE *rise)* Barry! I'm so glad you're back.

BARRY. And I'm glad you're still here, Gladys. I was afraid you might have left.

GLADYS. Oh, no!

PATSIE. She's still here—and so am I.

BARRY. *(Makes a wry face)* Er—yes—so I see.

MILLER. Young man, I trust this has been a lesson to you.

BARRY. *(Earnestly)* It has—it certainly has.

MILLER. No more kidnapings?

BARRY. Say, from now on, I'm going to be as industrious as a—I mean, no more kidnapings.

MILLER. I trust not.

MRS. LINDEN. *(Thrusting* PATSIE *forward)* Go on, Baby—tell him.

PATSIE. Barry, we're gonna get married—right away.

BARRY. Er—are we?

PATSIE. First thing tomorrow morning. *(With finality)* And I mean it.

BARRY. *(Takes a deep breath)* I'm sorry, Patsie— I—I can't marry you.

PATSIE. *(Belligerently)* And why can't you?

BARRY. Because I— *(Looks at* GLADYS; *she smiles radiantly at him and he braces himself)* Because I don't love you.

PATSIE. You said you did.

BARRY. I've changed my mind.

PATSIE. *(Indignantly)* Didn't you say I was your dream girl? Didn't you say you couldn't live without me?

BARRY. *(Winces)* That was a long time ago.

PATSIE. You said—

MRS. LINDEN. Aw, stop trying to argue with him, Baby. Talk's cheap. *(To* BARRY*)* You'll either marry her or else.

BARRY. Or else what?

MRS. LINDEN. Or else pay through the nose. She's got letters, see? Plenty of letters!

BARRY. I'm sorry. If you want to sue for breach of promise, I guess you'll just have to go ahead. I'll take a chance on it.

MRS. LINDEN. Chance? What kinda chance you think you got? Juries never did like millionaires. *(Rises)* Come on, Baby—we're not getting anywhere this way.

MILLER. *(Rises. He has been taking all this in with a smile)* Just a minute—

MRS. LINDEN. What 've you got to do with it?

MILLER. Plenty—plenty! Barry, I've been trying to keep this from you, but—

ANN. *(Rushes in* R.1) Oh, Barry! Is everything all right?

BARRY. Sure, sure, Ann!

ANN. *(Happily)* I'm so glad!

BARRY. *(Impatiently)* Uh-huh! Go on, Mr. Miller.

MILLER. The fact is, I hardly believe this young woman—or anyone else—will care to sue you for breach of promise, when they know the true facts. *(Pauses to let this sink in.)*

BARRY. *(Apprehensively)* What true facts?

MILLER. I've been trying to spare your feelings— I wanted to make things as easy as possible for you. But—young man, you haven't a penny.

BARRY. *(Stunned) Whaaat?*

(Exclamations of astonishment from the OTHERS.*)*

MILLER. You're broke.

BARRY. *(Weakly)* Broke?

MILLER. You're wiped out—clean—a pauper!

BARRY. But—but—how did it happen?

MILLER. As you know, your father's fortune was invested in shares of the Hollis Mill entirely—

BARRY. Yeah.

MILLER. Unfortunately, the mill's business has been declining steadily. And now, despite everything we have tried to do, it becomes necessary to file a petition of bankruptcy.

BARRY. But—but— *(Shakes his head dazedly)* You never let me know. I—I thought everything was—hunky-dory.

MILLER. You were too young to be of any help. I thought it best to spare your feelings—and your Aunt Sue's.

BARRY. *(A glimmer of hope)* There's this house.

MILLER. *(Shakes his head)* Mortgaged. It will have to be sold to satisfy the debts.

BARRY. *(Forlorn)* Then you mean—I'm *really* broke?

MILLER. *Really.* You haven't got a single, solitary cent beyond what may be in your personal bank account.

MRS. LINDEN. How much is that?

BARRY. *(Dejectedly)* Eleven dollars and a half.

PATSIE. Is all this on the level?

MILLER. Completely, I assure you.

MRS. LINDEN. I don't believe it, Baby. It's just a trick--a trick to get rid of us.

BARRY. I wish it were.

MILLER. Madame, are you doubting the truth of my statements?

MRS. LINDEN. Yeah, Sonnie. Since you ask me, I *am* doubtin' the truth of your statements. How do I know it's on the level?

MILLER. *(Frowns)* H'mm! *(Looks in his pocket; extracts a legal-looking document)* Perhaps this will convince you. *(Hands it to her)* Bank statement on the Hollis Mills.

MRS. LINDEN. *(Trying to make something of it)* What's it mean?

PATSIE. *(Looking over her shoulder)* Lookit! *(Eagerly)* The total here is fifty thousand bucks!

BARRY. Fifty thousand—?

MILLER. Yes, but unfortunately, that fifty thousand, if you will notice, is a *deficit.*

(Their faces fall.)

PATSIE. Oh!

BARRY. You mean I owe that much?

MILLER. That is correct.

ANN. *(Regretfully)* I'm *terribly* sorry, Barry.

BARRY. Thanks, Ann.,

MILLER. *(Crosses to arch)* This is probably the best thing that could happen to you, my boy--- Make you settle down to your responsibilities in life—

BARRY. *(Mournfully)* Yeah.

MILLER. See me in my office, and we'll go over the matter more thoroughly. And—er—perhaps I can see about helping you get a job, too.

BARRY. Thanks a lot.

MILLER. Goodnight! Goodnight, all! *(Exits C. to L.)*

BARRY. Well—that seems to be that.

ANN. *(Helpfully)* Perhaps it's not so bad. As Mr. Miller said—

BARRY. Aw, skip it, Ann.

ANN. *(Bites her lip)* I'm sorry.

PATSIE. What's the next train out of here—East?

BARRY. There's one at midnight, I think.

MRS. LINDEN. You ain't givin' up so easy, Baby?

PATSIE. Lissen, I'm sick and tired of millionaires, Mom. I wanna get back to Hoboken, where at least I'm appreciated.

MRS. LINDEN. *(Regretfully)* Three million bucks —gone with the wind! *(Reproachfully to* BARRY*)* It's a pity you couldn't 'a' paid more attention to your business.

BARRY. Yeah, it is.

MRS. LINDEN. *(Sighs)* Lookit all the corn cure I coulda bought with three million dollars.

PATSIE. *(Getting her hat from the console table and putting it on at mirror)* Ready, Mom?

MRS. LINDEN. *(Gets her hat and puts it on)* Where's the bags?

PATSIE. *(Indicating* L.*)* There—in the hall.

BARRY. Shall I have Furber give you a hand with them?

PATSIE. No, thanks. We ain't cripples.

MRS. LINDEN. We'll have to have a cab.

BARRY. Er—there's one at the corner. I noticed it as I came in.

PATSIE. Thanks. *(To* MRS. LINDEN*)* All set?

MRS. LINDEN. Yeah. *(Sighs)* I think I coulda liked it here. The food wasn't at all bad.

PATSIE. Forget it, Mom. Well—goodbye, Barry!

BARRY. Goodbye, Patsie!

PATSIE. In the future, you wanna think twice before you tell a girl you can't live without her.

BARRY. I will.

PATSIE. And the next time you save a girl's life from drowning—

BARRY. The next time—I won't.

MRS. LINDEN. Yeah, you better just stay away from the water, Sonnie.

PATSIE. Well—I'll be seeing you in the funnies. Goodbye!

BARRY. Goodbye, goodbye!

(PATSIE *and* MRS. LINDEN *exeunt* C. *to* L.)

BARRY. *(Turns happily to* GLADYS.) And now, Gladys—

GLADYS. *(Coolly)* And now?

ANN. I—I guess two's company. Excuse me. *(Turns quickly and rushes out* R.I.)

GLADYS. What's eating her?

BARRY. I don't know. But listen, Gladys, now that we're alone at last, I want to tell you—

GLADYS. That's all right. You don't have to explain to me.

BARRY. Explain? I wasn't going to explain. I only wanted to say—

GLADYS. *(Crosses to arch)* Save your breath. I'm leaving.

BARRY. *(Unbelievingly)* Leaving?

GLADYS. Yes, leaving. Now! Immediately!

BARRY. Why?

GLADYS. Well, really! Do I have to draw you a picture?

BARRY. Gladys—let me get this straight. You—*you* weren't after my money? Oh, no—not you, of all people—

GLADYS. You don't think so?

BARRY. You—you *couldn't.*

GLADYS. Well, what do you suppose I saw in you? Certainly not your brain.

BARRY. But—but—

GLADYS. And emphatically not your good looks!

BARRY. But—

GLADYS. Oh, stop imitating a goat. Listen to me. I've been poor all my life—poor as a church mouse, see? And when I marry, I'm going to *improve* myself—

BARRY. *(Stunned)* I—I see.

GLADYS. I'm certainly not going to throw away my whole future on a—a miserable bankrupt.

BARRY. You—you've got it all planned, haven't you?

GLADYS. Yes, I know exactly what I want—and I'm going to get it.

BARRY. You probably will. You're very—very efficient, aren't you?

GLADYS. Thanks.

BARRY. Cool as a cucumber, aren't you? When you met me on the train, you saw, not me, but three million dollars, isn't that it?

GLADYS. To put it bluntly, yes.

BARRY. And now that the three millions are **gone**, there's nothing to keep you, is there?

GLADYS. Do you blame me?

BARRY. *(Considers)* No—no, I suppose not. After all, I suppose it's just a—a *business* with you, and I don't blame you. *(Shakes his head)* Do you suppose there's anybody—in the whole world—who'd want me just for *myself?*

GLADYS. Personally, I think she'd be a sap to. A girl's got to look out for herself these days.

BARRY. That's right.

GLADYS. Well, so long!

BARRY. So long!

GLADYS. *(At console table, puts on her hat, gets her bag)* It was a nice dream while it lasted, wasn't it?

BARRY. Yes—a nice—dream.

GLADYS. Now I suppose I've got to start looking for another millionaire. *(Sighs)* That's the way life is.

BARRY. Oh, you'll find one—no doubt of that. With your determination, you're bound to get what you're looking for.

GLADYS. I'm going to keep trying, anyway. They can't shoot you for that, can they? Goodbye!

BARRY. Good luck! *(She exits* C. *to* L. BARRY, *deep in thought, comes down and sits in divan.)*

FURBER. *(After a moment, enters* R.I) Beg pardon, Mr. Barry. Is there something I can get you?

BARRY. No, thanks. (FURBER *turns to go)* Wait a minute. Is the cook around?

FURBER. Kathleen? She's been to the movies, sir. But I believe she just returned.

BARRY. Tell her to make some coffee—lots of coffee. I've got some thinking to do.

FURBER. Very good, sir.

BARRY. Is Ann still there?

FURBER. Er—yes, sir. Shall I tell her you wish to see her?

BARRY. Yeah—if you don't mind.

FURBER. Certainly, sir. *(Exits* R.I.*)*

(BARRY *rises; starts pacing back and forth.)*

ANN. *(After a moment, enters* R.I. *Looks around)* Your—"dream girl" gone?

BARRY. Yes, she's gone. *(Starts to laugh, softly at first, but it gets louder and louder, becoming almost hysterical.)*

ANN. *(Alarmed)* What's the matter? Barry!

BARRY. *(Quiets down; comes over to her)* I was just thinking—we're funny, aren't we?

ANN. "We"?

BARRY. All of us—people—the funniest things in life—that's us!

Ann. What are you talking about?

Barry. *(Fiercely)* Look—what are you doing here?

Ann. *(Backs away, looking at him curiously)* I—I don't know.

Barry. You heard Miller say my money was all gone, didn't you?

Ann. Yes.

Barry. Then what are you waiting for?

Ann. *(Flaring back)* You don't—you don't suppose *that* makes any difference to me?

Barry. You're not interested in my money?

Ann. Certainly I'm interested in it. I think you should have got rid of it long ago. I think it's the worst thing that ever happened to you. I think you might have been a *fairly* human sort of person without it—instead of the irresponsible, conceited, empty-headed—

Barry. Whoo!

Ann. *(Calming down)* I'm sorry—but you asked for it.

Barry. I certainly did. *(Looks at her wonderingly)* I never knew you felt so strongly about me—

Ann. *(Turns away)* Perhaps I shouldn't have said it—

Barry. I'm glad you did, Ann.

Ann. *(Crosses to R.1)* Excuse me—

Barry. Ann, wait! *(Quickly crosses to her)* I'm everything you said I was—and more. I've been a fool—a darn fool. And blind as a bat.

Ann. Have you?

Barry. *(Nods)* But I won't be any more—I promise—if you give me a chance.

Ann. Me?

Barry. *(Takes her hand)* Can't we be friends, Ann?

Ann. *(Looks away)* You're forgetting that I—

(RALPH *enters* R.I. BARRY *quickly drops her hand.*)

BARRY. *(Nervously)* Hello! Er—you still here?

RALPH. Yeah. And it seems I came in just in time.

ANN. Now, Ralph— Listen—

RALPH. You listen to me. I don't want you playing around with this cheap heel—

BARRY. Me?

RALPH. *(Belligerently)* Yeah, you! Wanna make something of it?

BARRY. Er—no, thanks.

RALPH. It's you and me for good, Ann, and I don't intend to let anything stop it. Get that?

ANN. And suppose I don't feel that way about it?

RALPH. You'd better feel that way about it— that's all I've got to say.

KATHLEEN. *(Enters* R.I *with a tray on which is the coffee)* Here's the coffee, sir.

BARRY. Oh, thanks, Kathleen! Just put it down there.

KATHLEEN. Yes, sir. *(Places tray on coffee table. RALPH, at the sight of KATHLEEN, has begun to sneak up to the arch. She looks up and sees him. Stands staring at him for a moment, unable to believe her eyes)* Glory be!

RALPH. *(All the starch gone out of him)* I-–er— I've got to go— *(Reaches arch.)*

KATHLEEN. By the living Saint Patrick, it's my Percival.

BARRY *and* ANN. *(Together) What?*

RALPH. I've got to go— Ha, ha! *(Laughs weakly)* Excuse me—

KATHLEEN. *(Suddenly galvanized into action)* Oh, no, you don't! *(Rushes up to arch; grabs him by the ear.)*

RALPH. Just a minute—there must be some mistake—

KATHLEEN. Mistake, is it? Well— *(Slaps him in the face)* That ain't no mistake.

RALPH. *(Cringing)* Don't! I can explain—

KATHLEEN. And you'll have the chance to, I'm thinking. You'll have the chance to do a whole heap of explaining, and it better be good—!

BARRY. Kathleen! This is the man who left you in Niagara Falls?

KATHLEEN. The same, sir—bad cess to him! *(Slaps him again.)*

RALPH. Stop! Don't!

(BARRY *and* ANN *laugh.*)

KATHLEEN. Stop, is it? *(Slaps him)* Don't, is it? *(Slaps him)* That's just a start, me buckaroo—just a start for the four years of worry and shame you brought me.

RALPH. But I—I thought you were dead.

KATHLEEN. Oh, you thought I was dead? *(Slaps him.)*

RALPH. I—I tried to find you.

KATHLEEN. You tried to find me? *(Slaps him.)*

RALPH. Kathleen! Stop! Listen to reason—

KATHLEEN. I'm listenin'. Is it something more you'd be after telling me now?

RALPH. *(Rubs his face)* Can't we—talk this over —in peace?

KATHLEEN. Peace, is it? *(Laughs grimly)* Mister, I'm thinking you won't be knowing the meaning of the word from now on. I thank the good Lord for answering my prayers at last— *(Leads him by the ear to door* R.1) Come along with you now. I wouldn't be after annoying *decent* people with the sight of a skunk like you—

RALPH. *(Squirming)* Now, Kathleen—

KATHLEEN. Now, Kathleen — now, Kathleen! *(Slaps him and pulls him out* R.1.)

BARRY. *(Laughing)* Well, that seems to take care of your friend Ralph, doesn't it?

ANN. And how!

BARRY. How did you ever get mixed up with him?

ANN. How did *you* ever get mixed up with—?

BARRY. *(Winces)* Never mind.

(WARN Curtain.)

ANN. Seriously, I never did care much for his company. But he was so persistent—followed me everywhere I'd go—refused to take "no" for an answer—

BARRY. *(Looking at her intently)* I can understand that.

ANN. Can you?

BARRY. *(Nods)* There's nothing to prevent us from being friends *now,* is there—?

ANN. Well— *(Considers)* For one thing, you'll have to be looking for a job—

BARRY. Oh, that! Ann—I have a little confession to make.

ANN. What?

BARRY. I'm not broke, after all.

ANN. You're *not? (He shakes his head)* But—but I heard Mr. Miller say—

BARRY. And he did a swell job of it, didn't he?

ANN. You mean—you put him up to it?

BARRY. Uh-huh! I thought it would be a good way of getting rid of Patsie—

ANN. And it turned out to be a good way of getting rid of Gladys, too.

BARRY. *(Winces)* Don't remind me of that—ever again—will you?

ANN. *(Smiles)* All right—I won't.

BARRY. You said I might have been fairly human without my money. Maybe I still can be, with it. If you'll help me. Will you?

ANN. *(Looks up at him)* I'll try.

BARRY. That's fine, Ann. You won't regret it. I'll turn over a new leaf. I'll be as industrious as a beaver. I'll never look at another girl again as long as I live—never.

THE CURTAIN FALLS

OH, PROMISE ME!

PROPERTY PLOT

Furishings:
Divan.
Coffee table.
Two end tables.
Library table.
Desk.
Three armchairs.
Desk chair.
Two torchieres.
Two table lamps.
Console table.
Mirror.
Telephone.
Large pottery vase.
Rug, on floor.
Curtains, drapes, on windows.
Pictures, on walls.
Books, ashtrays, etc.

Hand Properties:
  Act I, Scene I:
Flowers (FURBER).
Watch (MILLER).
Newspaper (on desk).
Several pieces of baggage (FURBER).
Man's hat (on console table).
Tea-wagon (KATHLEEN).
Sandwiches

Cups
Saucers
Cream
Sugar
Napkin
On tea-wagon.
Sheet of notepaper (MRS. HOLLIS).
Percolator with coffee (KATHLEEN).
Pen (on desk).
Paper (on desk).
Envelopes (on desk).
Address book (BARRY).

Act I, Scene II:
Tea-wagon (FURBER).
Two cups of coffee (on tea-wagon).
Napkins (on tea-wagon).
Purse (PATSIE).
Purse (MRS. HOLLIS).
Bill (MRS. HOLLIS).
Several pieces of luggage (FURBER).
Letter (PATSIE).

Act II:
"Baby," a life-size doll wrapped in blankets
    (BARRY).
Overnight bag (GLADYS).
Revolver (RALPH).

Act III:
Three lady's hats (on console table).
Overnight bag (in hall).
Book (GLADYS).
Revolver (RALPH).
Handkerchief (RALPH).
Watch (MILLER).
Document (MILLER).
Tray, with cup of coffee (KATHLEEN).

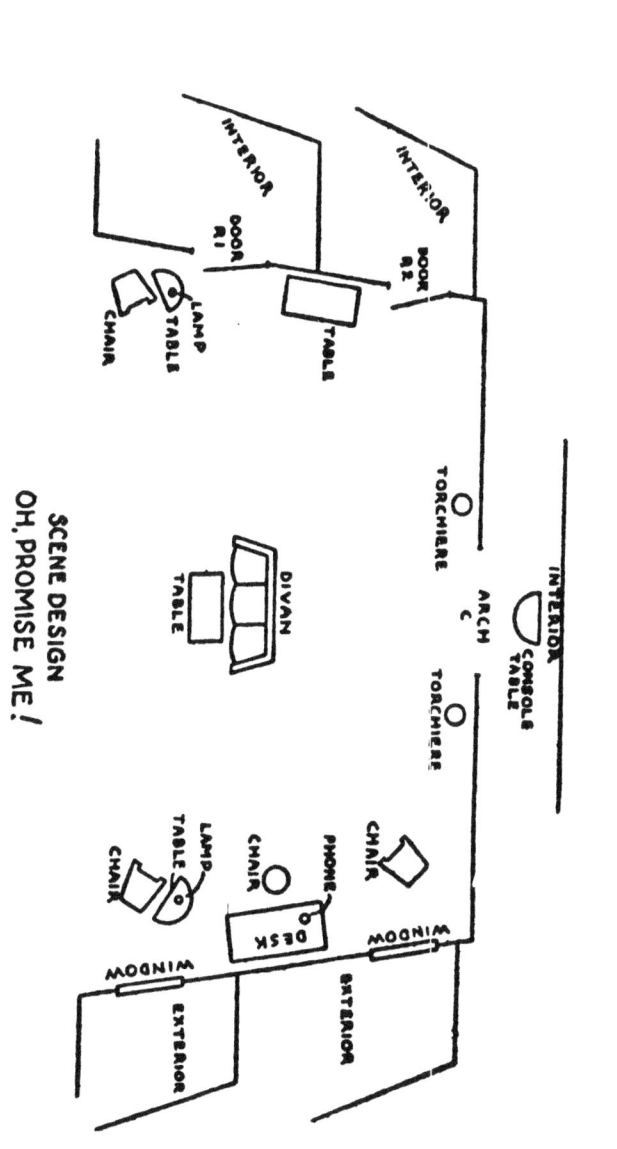

SCENE DESIGN

OH, PROMISE ME!

SKIN DEEP
Jon Lonoff

Comedy / 2m, 2f / Interior Unit Set

In *Skin Deep*, a large, lovable, lonely-heart, named Maureen Mulligan, gives romance one last shot on a blind-date with sweet awkward Joseph Spinelli; she's learned to pepper her speech with jokes to hide insecurities about her weight and appearance, while he's almost dangerously forthright, saying everything that comes to his mind. They both know they're perfect for each other, and in time they come to admit it.

They were set up on the date by Maureen's sister Sheila and her husband Squire, who are having problems of their own: Sheila undergoes a non-stop series of cosmetic surgeries to hang onto the attractive and much-desired Squire, who may or may not have long ago held designs on Maureen, who introduced him to Sheila. With Maureen particularly vulnerable to both hurting and being hurt, the time is ripe for all these unspoken issues to bubble to the surface.

"Warm-hearted comedy … the laughter was literally show-stopping. A winning play, with enough good-humored laughs and sentiment to keep you smiling from beginning to end."
- TalkinBroadway.com

"It's a little Paddy Chayefsky, a lot Neil Simon and a quick-witted, intelligent voyage into the not-so-tranquil seas of middle-aged love and dating. The dialogue is crackling and hilarious; the plot simple but well-turned; the characters endearing and quirky; and lurking beneath the merriment is so much heartache that you'll stand up and cheer when the unlikely couple makes it to the inevitable final clinch."
- NYTheatreWorld.Com

THE OFFICE PLAYS
Two full length plays by Adam Bock

THE RECEPTIONIST
Comedy / 2m, 2f / Interior

At the start of a typical day in the Northeast Office, Beverly deals effortlessly with ringing phones and her colleague's romantic troubles. But the appearance of a charming rep from the Central Office disrupts the friendly routine. And as the true nature of the company's business becomes apparent, The Receptionist raises disquieting, provocative questions about the consequences of complicity with evil.

"...Mr. Bock's poisoned Post-it note of a play."
- New York Times

"Bock's intense initial focus on the routine goes to the heart of *The Receptionist's* pointed, painfully timely allegory... elliptical, provocative play..."
- Time Out New York

THE THUGS
Comedy / 2m, 6f / Interior

The Obie Award winning dark comedy about work, thunder and the mysterious things that are happening on the 9th floor of a big law firm. When a group of temps try to discover the secrets that lurk in the hidden crevices of their workplace, they realize they would rather believe in gossip and rumors than face dangerous realities.

"Bock starts you off giggling, but leaves you with a chill."
- Time Out New York

"... a delightfully paranoid little nightmare that is both more chillingly realistic and pointedly absurd than anything John Grisham ever dreamed up."
- New York Times

SAMUELFRENCH.COM

NO SEX PLEASE, WE'RE BRITISH
Anthony Marriott and Alistair Foot

Farce / 7 m, 3 f / Interior

A young bride who lives above a bank with her husband who is the assistant manager, innocently sends a mail order off for some Scandinavian glassware. What comes is Scandinavian pornography. The plot revolves around what is to be done with the veritable floods of pornography, photographs, books, films and eventually girls that threaten to engulf this happy couple. The matter is considerably complicated by the man's mother, his boss, a visiting bank inspector, a police superintendent and a muddled friend who does everything wrong in his reluctant efforts to set everything right, all of which works up to a hilarious ending of closed or slamming doors. This farce ran in London over eight years and also delighted Broadway audiences.

"Titillating and topical."
- "NBC TV"

"A really funny Broadway show."
- "ABC TV"

WHITE BUFFALO
Don Zolidis

Drama / 3m, 2f (plus chorus)/ Unit Set

Based on actual events, WHITE BUFFALO tells the story of the miracle birth of a white buffalo calf on a small farm in southern Wisconsin. When Carol Gelling discovers that one of the buffalo on her farm is born white in color, she thinks nothing more of it than a curiosity. Soon, however, she learns that this is the fulfillment of an ancient prophecy believed by the Sioux to bring peace on earth and unity to all mankind. Her little farm is quickly overwhelmed with religious pilgrims, bringing her into contact with a culture and faith that is wholly unfamiliar to her. When a mysterious businessman offers to buy the calf for two million dollars, Carol is thrown into doubt about whether to profit from the religious beliefs of others or to keep true to a spirituality she knows nothing about.

www.ingramcontent.com/pod-product-compliance
Lightning Source LLC
Chambersburg PA
CBHW070639120726
47909CB00004B/1500